PERFECT BLOOD

INNOCENT BLOOD

"And the wild regrets, and the bloody sweats
None knew so well as I
For he who lives more lives than one
More deaths than one must die."

Oscar Wilde
The Ballad of Reading Gaol

"For we wrestle not against flesh and blood . . ."

Ephesians 6:12.

ONE

Icy slush filled Deirdre's sneakers and soaked the hem of her faded jeans as she stepped out of the car. "Thanks for the ride, Phil. If you pop open the trunk, I'll just get my stuff."

"No problem, I'm at your service." Phil bounced out, slamming the door and brandishing his keys. He opened the trunk and grabbed Deirdre's shopping bags.

"Thanks." She reached for them, but he swung them out of her reach and headed for the door. Leave it to Phil to make the gentlemanly gesture while keeping his Gucci loafers dry—the puddle was on her side of the car.

He smirked. "I said I'm at your service—and that's door-to-door."

"Phil, it's late and I'm tired. We both have work tomorrow. Let's just say good night." Streetlights gleamed on sleet-coated the sidewalks. As a bitter gust rounded the corner, she pulled up the collar on her navy pea coat and reached again for the bags.

"So after all I did for you — drive you to the mall, buy you dinner, take you to work and drive you home — you aren't even going to invite me up to your apartment for a drink?" Phil shrugged and moved closer with an ingratiating smile.

"I don't have anything to drink."

"Not even a glass of water?"

Deirdre heard sirens approaching a neighboring street, a wailing counterpoint to her uncharitable thoughts. She shuddered. "Phil, please let me go."

"Not till you thank me properly." He dropped her parcels and leaned closer, backing her up against the door. "Just a little kiss?"

"No!" Deirdre pushed him futilely, but his hands pressed against the glass, trapping her.

"May I help?"

Deirdre looked up. A wide brimmed hat shaded the face of a tall stranger in a long, dark coat. She shivered, hugging herself, and glared at Phil.

"Shall I summon the police?" He held out his cell phone, his thumb poised over the keypad.

"Yes, please," she decided.

"No, thanks," spat Phil. "I'm out of here." He scurried to his BMW, spinning the tires as he pulled into the street.

Deirdre fumbled for her shopping bags and tried to blink back furious tears. She didn't want to meet the stranger's eyes and she wondered if he would leave.

"Allow me." He inserted his key in the lock and held the door open.

"Thank you. I think you saved my life. Literally."

"Well, you can see I had a vested interest—you were blocking the door."

She glanced up in time to catch a glimmer of a smile. "I suppose we were. It's a good thing you came along when you did."

"Damsel-in-distress is not my usual line of work, but I'm glad I did, too."

The door clicked behind them enveloping them in warmth and the smell of the old leather chairs and dusty ficus trees that furnished the lobby. Deirdre sorted her belongings and retrieved her keys.

The stranger lingered. "Can I help you with those bags?"

"No, I've got them, thanks." She paused. "No offense."

"None taken. You're probably wise not to trust a stranger in the middle of the night." He headed for the elevator.

Deirdre was going that way too. "At least you live in the building. I'm surprised we haven't met before, but then I do work evenings."

"So do I," he replied. "I DJ a nighttime program at the classical radio station—eight to midnight, Monday through Friday. A Little Night Music—maybe you've heard of it?"

She shook her head. "Oh, sorry, I haven't. That's when I work. I guess I'd be home before the end, but I usually go right to bed."

"And I just happen to be one of the children of the night. I sleep by day and roam the darkened streets. But what about you? You're not wearing scrubs so you can't be a nurse. Where do you work at night?"

"At the Union Square Theater. I'm the wardrobe mistress. That's where I met Phil—he's one of the actors." She watched as her companion pushed the call button for the elevator. "I just wanted a ride to the mall—Christmas shopping, you know—then he bought me dinner and drove me back to work. He seemed to think that entitled him to . . . to . . . oh, I don't know . . . more than I wanted to offer."

"I understand. I've known a few people like that myself."

She smiled at him. "I don't know why I'm unburdening myself to a stranger."

"Because you're upset. It's natural to want to talk things over."

"And I don't have anyone at home to talk to." She sighed. "Still, I apologize for taking advantage."

"Not at all. In fact, it's a pleasure to meet a neighbor. I'm such a night bird; I don't get to see many of the others in the building." The elevator came and he held the door as she loaded in her bags. "Would you prefer to ride up alone? I can wait for the elevator to return."

"Oh, no, you can come." It seemed rude to make him wait after all he had done, but just the same, uncomfortable being alone in a box with an unknown man, Deirdre moved to the far corner. As she reached for the floor button, she noticed the number he had already pressed. "You live on the sixth floor, too?"

"For the last five years."

"I've been here four months, but they've been a little hectic. No wonder we haven't met."

"Well, now that we know where each other live, perhaps we'll meet again." He stopped by unit 609.

She chuckled. "We're sure to—my apartment is across the hall—610."

"Since you are home safe, I'll wish you fare well, until next time."

"How about this weekend?" Deirdre wondered if an edge of desperation had touched her voice, but it was too late to stop. "If you haven't seen the show at the theater, I can get you tickets—free. We get comps for every show. *The Importance of Being Earnest* is running now. You said you don't work Saturdays."

"I'd like that. Would you permit me to take you to dinner afterwards? With no further expectations, of course."

Deirdre blushed. "That sounds nice. The show starts at seven o'clock. I'll leave a ticket for you at the box office."

"I'll see you then." He turned to his own door.

"Wait. I need to know your name."

"Benton Colyer." He swept off his hat and made a bow. "Most people call me Ben."

She pretended to curtsey. "I'm Deirdre Maguire."

Benton waited as she unlocked her door. She turned to wave, but paused at the inscrutable look on his face. "Until tomorrow, then."

He nodded. "Good night."

* * * *

Benton opened his door and stepped into his apartment. *Close your heart, Benton, don't get involved.* He shut the door, leaned against it and looked around the room. His apartment was furnished comfortably, but sparingly; no books or photographs cluttered the surfaces. He preferred it that way—no personal accoutrements, no personal entanglements. Some of his colleagues called him a hermit, but he had always enjoyed his single status until tonight.

Somehow, this brief conversation had awoken a need for companionship. He thought of the tone in her voice as she offered tickets, the wistful look on her face as she closed her door. He was surprised by the attraction he felt to her, and by the fact that he had made a date.

Surely one date couldn't hurt.

TWO

"Rhonda, I need a ticket for tonight," Deirdre called through the box office window.

Rhonda turned from sorting the rack of tickets, and tucked her long hair behind her ears. "Get out! So, do you finally have a date or what?"

"I guess you could call it a date." Deirdre shrugged. "He's just a guy I met in my building last night. He practically snatched me out of Phil's clutches. So I said I'd get him a ticket and he said he'd take me to supper after."

"That is definitely a date, Deirdre. I'm so happy for you. It's about time you found yourself a boyfriend." She dragged a stool over to the window and sat down.

"Oh, Rhonda, he's hardly my boyfriend—I told you we just met the other night."

7

Rhonda leaned on her elbows. "Go on—tell me all about it."

"There's not much to tell." Deirdre counted on her fingers. "One. Phil had me backed into a corner. Two. This man came along in the nick of time. I must say, it was refreshing to meet someone polite for a change."

"Is he cute?"

"I guess so. He's tall, with a long coat and a big hat." She gestured with her hands. "Actually he was a little mysterious."

"Wow, that is so romantic." Rhonda sighed and rolled her eyes. "You are so lucky to catch a guy like that."

"Slow down, Rhonda, I hardly know him. We only talked for a minute."

"Okay. Maybe he's not a boyfriend now, he's definitely in the running."

"Come off it." Deirdre flapped her hands. "How many times do I have to tell you I am not in the market for a boyfriend? I have enough on my plate with guys like Phil. Thank goodness he's only in this one play."

Rhonda reached under the bottom of the glass divider with a carefully manicured hand and patted Deirdre's arm. "I know some of these actors are hard to work with—and back stage you're the one who has to take the brunt. But that's all the more reason to have a real boyfriend on the side—one who has a normal life."

"Well, his life's not all that normal—he hosts an evening radio show."

"Really? What did you say his name was?"

"Benton Colyer."

"You're kidding, right?"

"Why, do you know him?"

"I don't know him; I know *of* him. He's—like—a local celebrity. I listen to him all the time. He has the sexiest voice—smooth and low with just a hint of the south." Rhonda patted herself on the chest, just over her heart. "Someone with a voice like that has to be either totally adorable, or really gross. You *must* have noticed."

"I told you—he wasn't overwhelmingly hideous or anything like that." She frowned a little in thought. "I wasn't paying a lot of attention. I did have other things on my mind."

"The girl meets Benton Colyer, and she isn't paying attention. Deirdre, you're hopeless." Rhonda shook her head, dislodging a strand of hair. "You'll never get a man if you don't pay attention."

"And I told you, I'm not looking for a man."

"But if you don't start paying a little attention sometime, you'll shrivel into an old maid." Rhonda leaned close to the glass. "At least give this guy a chance. He sounds nice."

Deirdre leaned closer, whispering, "You just like him 'cause he's famous."

"Yeah, well, you just like him 'cause he's polite!"

"All right—you win. And anyway, I *am* giving him a chance—dinner tonight. Then we'll see. Save him a ticket. You'll have to judge for yourself if he's cute."

Rhonda sighed. "Well, at least that's a start."

9

Deirdre made the most of the time between costume changes to apply some makeup and borrow a curling iron. Maybe she didn't want a "boyfriend," but she did want to make a good impression. She hoped jeans and a sweater would be suitable for the restaurant they were going to. She could have changed her clothes, but there was always some tidying up to do after all the actors left. She didn't want to keep Benton waiting after the curtain came down any more than absolutely necessary.

She gave a last check in the mirror. Her unruly hair stayed captured in a bun for once, and her favorite sweater did its usual flattering magic. She tried to cool her fiery cheeks with cold hands, but she couldn't slow her racing heart. This time she would be sure to pay attention.

She found Ben in the green room admiring the sludgy coffee steaming in the bottom of the pot. He looked to her like a character from an old monochromatic movie. Without his hat and coat, she noticed his crisp, gray flannel trousers and black cashmere sweater. His hair was black; it hung to his shoulders, curling around his white face. Even his eyes were gray. Deirdre grinned—Rhonda would have to agree he was handsome.

"Good evening," he said giving her an appreciative smile.

"Hi." She pointed to the coffeepot. "You didn't drink any of that, did you?"

"No. Does anyone?"

"It's the remains of the batch the stage manager makes at half hour."

"Half hour? What's that?" he asked.

"Sorry, I forgot you're one of the uninitiated. That's half-hour before the curtain rises. All the actors have to be here by then. Some of them like coffee while they put on their make-up. Then the leftovers sit there the rest of the night. I personally won't touch it after eight o'clock."

He set the carafe back on the burner and shut it off. "I'm not a big coffee drinker, but the place I'm taking you makes good espresso, if you happen to like that. I guarantee it's better than this!"

"Sounds great. I'll get my coat and bag."

He took her jacket and held it while she slipped her arms into the sleeves.

Luigi's restaurant was cozy; candles glowed on each table and a row of booths in the back made room for private conversations away from the bustle of the late-night crowd. A waitress led them to one of these, brought them napkins, menus and, at Ben's suggestion, espresso.

He raised his cup. "Thank you for the ticket. I enjoyed the show."

"You're welcome. I can get tickets for you anytime. I'm not from around here, so the people I know all work at the theater—to be honest you're the only acquaintance I have who would use them." She felt her cheeks grow warm and sipped some coffee to cover her boldness.

The waitress brought tossed salads and a basket of warm garlic knots.

"I understand these are a specialty of the house," he passed the basket to Deirdre, "but could I have plain rolls?"

"Of course," The waitress replied, "I'll bring some right away."

Benton seasoned his salad with oil and vinegar. "Would you let me take you to dinner again? It's the least I can do in exchange for a ticket."

"You don't have to do anything. I told you the tickets are free." She forked up a bite of salad.

His eyes twinkled. "But it's a good way to get to know you."

She grinned. "In that case, I accept."

"Good." He took her hand. She curled her fingers around his, stroking his smooth skin, white and cool as marble.

"You're paler than I am," she noticed. "Don't you ever go out in the sun?"

He slipped his hand away.

"Not if I can help it. I told you, I thrive in the moonlight." He scowled at someone crossing the room. "Uh oh."

"Well. Well. What have we here?"

Deirdre looked up. A young man lounged over the back of the booth.

"Benton Colyer—where have you been keeping yourself?" he asked.

When Ben didn't answer, the young man jabbed Deirdre in the shoulder. "Benton knows *all* the night spots, but he hasn't been here for weeks. I feel snubbed."

Deirdre rubbed the spot where he poked her.

Ben sighed. "Hello, Sidell."

"Thanks, I'd love to join you." He slid onto the bench next to Ben and beckoned to the waitress for another coffee. "So—who's this?"

Deirdre flushed again under his assessing gaze and bit into the fragrant garlic bread.

"Deirdre, may I introduce Sidell Prentis, an old . . . friend. Sidell, this is Deirdre Maguire." Ben's formal tone seemed to be strictly for business.

"A new friend, I presume." He flicked a lock of sleek blond hair off his brow and sipped his coffee.

"My dinner companion."

"Ahh, I see." His smile seemed more of a knowing smirk.

Ben scowled. "Come on, Sid, don't you have something else to do?"

"Something better than spend the evening with you and your lovely companion?" He planted his elbows squarely on the table. "I do not."

Sidell opened a menu. "What are you having? The veal is always good."

"Not for you." Benton retrieved the menu. "You're intruding—now, will you please leave?"

Sidell put an arm around Benton's shoulders. "I'm hurt. I just got here and you want me to go."

Ben brushed away the arm and tried to shove him out of the seat. Sidell held his ground, smiling oddly.

13

A glass of water tipped and rolled to the floor, shattering.

Deirdre saw the owner hurrying over, concern creasing his forehead. "Ben, don't spoil the evening with a fight. It's okay with me if he stays."

Ben retreated to the corner of the booth and soothed the owner. "I'm sorry if we disturbed anyone. It seems that my friend is hungry."

The owner bowed as he straightened the table and signaled for a busboy to pick up the glass. "You'll have your dinner right away."

The arrival of dinner eased the atmosphere for a while. The food was delicious—especially the veal—but as she reeled in a bite of spaghetti, Deirdre sensed Ben's annoyance and Sidell's enjoyment.

A typical vicious triangle coiled around the table. Ben wanted Sid to leave. Sid wanted her to leave. Deirdre wanted to stay with Ben. At a loss for how to handle the awkward situation, she fell back on the traditional standby—small talk.

"So, Sidell, you and Ben are old friends?"

"Oh yes. We've known each other for *years*. Doesn't it seem like that, Benton?" He raised a slender eyebrow.

"It's been a long time," Ben agreed.

Sidell continued, "Back then, there were rumors of war, jobs were hard to find, and I found myself without a place to live.

"In desperation I would have chosen to drug my excremental existence, but lucky for me, I found Benton. Or perhaps I should say, Benton found me.

He took me off the street and—eventually—showed me a better way."

Sidell turned and looked at Ben. "I suppose the world was a different place back then, but really the funny old world doesn't change much in the long run. Isn't that right, Benton?"

"No, Sidell, it doesn't." Ben scowled, slumped with his arms crossed in the corner of the booth.

Sidell folded his napkin and stood up. "Well, I must leave you two. It's been, in its own way, delightful. Remember what I said, my dear: Benton showed me a better way." He strode across the room.

"I apologize, I'm being a boor." Ben rubbed his face, sighed, then took Deirdre's hand. "I'm sorry you had to sit through that. Sid enjoys a little scene now and then."

"I didn't really mind," she said politely.

He looked surprised. "But I did. I asked you out for a quiet dinner, not some kind of *ménage a trois*. Please let me make it up to you another night."

"All right. If you insist, I would like that." She still had her hand wrapped in his.

"Now, would you like some dessert?"

"No thanks—it's late and I need to get *some* sleep tonight."

"Then I'll take you home."

They had walked to the restaurant from the theater, so now they started walking home. Deirdre savored the clear night air, admiring the star-crusted sky above them. She took Ben's arm as he strode confidently through the streets.

"Do you always walk at night?" she asked.

"Yes. It's hard to get a taxi, and the busses don't run this late. Besides, this is my home, I like to walk."

"So do I, but I worry sometimes about being out on my own. Aren't you afraid of getting mugged?"

"I never think of it."

She frowned at the blunt answer, but he smiled, spreading the skirts of his long, black overcoat. "Don't I look like someone best left to his own devices?"

"Yes, you do. In fact . . ."

"In fact, that's what you thought when we first met. Right?"

She nodded. "Yes, I confess, for a moment I did. But in that case, don't the police think *you're* a mugger?"

"When I first moved to this town, they used to question me from time to time, and once I spent a night in jail, but now I'm a familiar sight. They smile, wave, and leave me alone." Ben pulled out his key and opened the apartment house door. "Here we are."

"Thanks," she said as he held the door. "And thank you for a nice evening. I enjoyed myself."

"You're welcome. So did I. Again, I apologize for Sidell."

"He was . . . interesting." She puzzled. "There's something about him."

"Indeed there is." Benton sighed and she detected a note of frustration. "All the same, I'd prefer to leave him out of the equation next time."

16

"Well, me too." She held out her hand.

"Until then." He took her fingers and bowed. "Sleep well, Deirdre."

"You, too."

They turned to their own apartments.

Deirdre undressed and snuggled into bed. *Next time?* He hadn't said when that would be, but she hoped he wouldn't wait long. She smiled at the thought of seeing him regularly. It might be nice to have a boyfriend after all.

Rhonda will tease me no end when she hears that. Deirdre drifted to sleep.

THREE

Deirdre wrapped a fuzzy scarf around her neck and hoisted her tote bag onto her shoulder, ready for work. She buttoned her pea coat and checked the pockets for her gloves and keys. She trudged down the empty carpet-lined corridor and punched the elevator call button, wondering when she'd see Benton again. It had only been a day since they had gone out, but she longed to see him, to share the jokes of the day with him, to find out what it was like to work at a radio station. Tapping her foot, she watched the numbers descend. The doors slid open and she stepped out.

"Deirdre."

She jumped. Benton was standing behind her. "Where did you come from?"

He put out a hand to steady her. "I've been waiting for you—I saw you leave your apartment, and here I am."

"You weren't in the elevator—how'd you get down here so fast?"

He chuckled. "The elevator is not the only way down."

"But . . ."

He took her arm. "Will you permit me to walk you to work?"

"Why, yes." She looked around, still puzzled by Benton's arrival. "But I was planning to go to the farmers' market first. It's open today and I haven't had a chance to explore it before now."

"Then it would be my pleasure to introduce you to its many delights." He led the way.

Deirdre held his hand as they picked their way between crates of oranges and lettuce and inhaled a heady mixture of spices, floral arrangements and frying burgers.

"This is amazing. I didn't know they had clothes here—or books." She paused at a table of second-hand hardcover editions priced at five dollars. "It's hard to resist."

Benton blew the dust off a volume of stories by Nathaniel Hawthorne. "Are you looking for something specific?"

She tore herself away from the bookseller. "Spices and dried fruit—for holiday baking."

"This way." He steered her through the crowd.

"What are those?" She stopped and pointed to a display of strange-looking red objects hanging over the butcher's booth.

"Rabbits," he answered.

"Oh." She stared. "They're . . . dead. It's the whole rabbit."

"Yes." Ben licked his lips. "Don't they look nice and juicy?"

"I don't know—I've never eaten rabbit. I wouldn't even know how to cook one." She shrugged, and looked at Ben.

"I don't know how to cook them either." He gazed a moment longer at the rabbits, finally turning with a smile. "Let's find those spices you wanted."

Deirdre chose the spices she needed as well as a couple that Benton recommended. She added raisins and apricots to the selection, and then walnuts and almonds. Ben chose hazelnuts and dried peaches. Laden down, they headed for the burger stand. Deirdre snagged a table while Ben ordered burgers and fries for them both. As she piled their coats and packages on an extra chair, she noticed the hem had ripped out of one of his coat sleeves and a button was missing.

She picked it up. "I can fix this for you."

"Don't bother. It's not a big deal." He took the coat and folded it on the chair.

But this was her area. "It's no bother, Ben. It's what I do all the time. Bring the coat upstairs when we get to the theater. I promise it will only take a minute. Besides, it's a good coat—if you keep it repaired, it will last forever."

"Forever—hmm." He shook his head. "It's old enough as it is."

Deirdre fingered the thick felt-like wool. "It's beautiful. A coat like this costs a fortune these days. It looks so turn-of-the-century. Did you get it at a thrift store?"

"No, I had it made."

"Oh, that accounts for the period look then."

"Well . . . yes, I guess it does." He handed her one of the burgers. "Do you like catsup or Tabasco sauce on your fries?" He liberally spiced his potatoes.

"Catsup." She reached for the other bottle.

"Delicious. It looks like blood." He scooped a blob from her plate with his finger and licked it off.

She laughed. "Ben, did anyone ever tell you that you're weird?"

"I don't think they did, but I truly am." He smiled, chuckled and then joined her laughing. "We should get going. You have a button to sew, and I have a promo to record."

Snow began to fall as they walked across town. The sidewalks were wet, not slippery yet, but the feathery flakes softened edges, brightening shadowed corners and dark stonework.

"There it is—Union Square Theater," Deirdre announced, pointing to the castle-like structure gleaming spot-lit in the evening.

"The Athenaeum."

"Yes. That's what it was called when it was new—"

"—in 1897. I remember when . . . er . . . I read about it. When they had the centennial celebration." He pulled his hat down as he gazed at the façade of multi-colored bricks.

"Come on." She took his hand. "I'll give you a mini-tour. That's the main entrance under the marquee with the flood light, but I always go in the side here."

She led him into the building, pointing out the offices, scene shop and prop shop. "There's storage under the stage, and a trap in case someone needs to appear out of the floor. There's a bar and restaurant down another level, and all the storage and kitchens for them, but I've never explored that far."

They climbed a double flight of stairs and she unlocked a door. "Here's the costume shop. Give me your coat and sit down. It will just take a moment."

"Yes, ma'am." He smiled as he handed her his coat, but he didn't sit. He prowled the room, looking in the corners and cupboards, touching the walls, finally stopping at the window. "I like the view."

"I do too. You can't see the big skyscrapers or modern buildings, so I like to imagine this view isn't all that different from when the building was built."

"A few changes, perhaps a bit more neon, but you're right. It's comforting." He sighed. "Are you done with my coat? I have to get going."

"Here it is." She reached for a garment brush to whisk away a few threads, but he took the coat from her hands.

"I really appreciate it." He slid his arms into the sleeves. "Oh, it's nice to have that hem fixed—thanks. It was more annoying that I realized."

"You're welcome. Like I said, it's my job."

"You don't have to show me out, I know the way."

"See you tomorrow then?" she asked.

He paused at the door. "Yes. Tomorrow."

He pulled the door shut behind him and he was gone.

* * * *

"I told you so." Rhonda shoved her arms into her ski jacket and poked her fingers into her gloves. "If anyone needed a guy, it was you. Now, tell me everything—where do you go? What do you do?"

"It's only been a couple of times, you know. I told you about the night I got him the ticket and we went out to dinner." Deirdre slung her bag over her shoulder as they headed out the door.

Rhonda nodded. "Go on."

"The next day he walked me to work. I was on my way to the farmer's market, so he came along and we had burgers at the stand in there. It wasn't really a *date*, but it was fun. Then I met him at the radio station one night after work. I got a tour of the studio and I watched for a while from the booth. Then we walked home. Nothing really special."

"Hmm. That's good for a start. You should make dinner for him some night."

"Cook for him? At home? Deirdre sensed Ben had a need for privacy.

"Hey, girl, these days you've got to be pushy. You want him to know you're interested, right?" Rhonda raised her eyebrows. "If he has to make all the moves,

24

he'll get bored and move on to the next girl. Trust me on this one."

"You make it sound like you've had a lot of boyfriends."

"Oh sure. Since high school?" Rhonda counted on her fingers. "Ten, maybe fifteen."

Deirdre groaned. She could count two or three. "That sounds like a lot. What happened?"

Her friend gave a casual shrug, flipping her long hair. "Well, like I said, either they get bored and move on, or I do."

"Oh, Rhonda, that's kind of sad. Don't you want something lasting?"

"Trust me, Dee, nothing in this world lasts. Besides, I'm out there, meeting guys, having a few laughs. It's not so bad. You should give it a try. And if you don't keep trying, you'll let the good one get away."

They stopped at the corner, stamping snow from their feet as the bus slowed to a stop. Deirdre thought Benton was probably one of the good ones.

"Here's my bus, got to go." Rhonda gave Deirdre a quick hug. "Don't let Benton get away. He sounds like a keeper to me."

Deirdre waved at the retreating bus.

"Hello, Deirdre." Sidell emerged from the alley. "Remember me?"

"Sidell. Of course I do." She dug her hands into her pockets.

"I thought I'd walk you home."

"Well . . . no, thanks, I'm fine on my own." As she noticed the strangely empty street, an ambulance wailed by.

"Whatever you like." He shrugged.

She strode briskly away, looking back as she got to the corner, but she couldn't see him. She blew out a breath of relief and hurried on. At the next block, she had to wait for the light to change. As she crossed the street, she found him leaning against the light post.

Oh, God, what do I do? He's stalking me.

Sidell smiled. "The dark alleys can be a short cut."

"I prefer to stay in the light." She tried to pass him, but he blocked her way.

"Snub me if you like, it makes no difference. You can't escape from me. I know where you live—Chestnut Street, in the same building as Benton."

"Oh." She shuddered at the thought of Sidell in her home. "Did he tell you that?"

"Of course not—I followed you home the other night. And I've been watching ever since. You aren't frightened, are you?"

Maybe frightened was too strong a word, but she was certainly apprehensive. As her fingers encountered her keys in her pocket, Deirdre remembered a self-protection tip and pushed the keys between her fisted fingers. She wondered if she would be able to use this improvised brass knuckle.

He took a firm grasp of her elbow. "I don't know why you should be worried. It's not as if I were a complete stranger. Now, come along with me."

"What do you want?" She pulled her arm from his grip.

"How perceptive! Naturally I want something. But only information. Simply tell me about you and Benton. You can do that, can't you?" He began to walk, gripping her arm again and forcing her to keep up.

She tried to pull free. "There isn't anything to tell—I've only known him a couple of weeks."

"Come now, I know Benton better than that. Don't you sleep with him?"

She frowned. "Of course not! We're just friends."

A strange smile crossed Sidell's face. "I see . . ."

"It's really none of your business. I don't want to talk about it anymore." She disengaged her arm, but he snatched her hand, twisting it painfully.

"Not my business? Well—I think it will be my business."

"Ouch!" *Sweet Jesus, help me.* Deirdre let go of the keys and grabbed the cross she wore on a chain around her neck.

Sidell dropped her hand, shaking his as if it were burned, then leaned so close his forehead almost touched hers. "Wait and see, my dear, wait and see."

She ran down the street, rubbing her sore wrist. This time, he made no attempt to follow, but stood at the corner. As she came to the apartment entryway, she looked back. He raised a hand, waving, then turned and strode away.

No wonder Ben doesn't like him. She shivered as she poked her key into the lock and opened the door.

But what in the world did he mean by "wait and see?"

* * * *

Performance time on Sunday was afternoon. If Deirdre attended Mass in the morning, she had to rush to the theater in time to pre-set the afternoon show. She barely had time to chew her lunch. The evening service at church offered a relaxed solution.

The small congregation had an intimate feel and most of the people sat near the front. Deirdre didn't mingle, but she had a favorite seat by the windows, bright even at night, from the outside lighting that flooded the church. She liked to read the inscriptions and think about what kind of person the donor might have been.

That night she sat daydreaming about Benton and wondering about the strange encounter with Sidell until long past the end of the service.

"May I help you with something, my child?" The priest leaned over the pew.

Deirdre turned. "No, I'm fine thank you." As she stood up, she noticed the sanctuary had emptied. "Oh, I'm sorry. I hope I haven't kept you waiting."

"Not long at all. Don't give it a second thought. I'm Father More, by the way."

"Deirdre Maguire." She shook his outstretched hand.

"I noticed you've been here the last couple of weeks. Are you new in town?"

"I've been working at the theater about four months."

"Union Square Theater?"

"Yes."

"How fascinating. I don't subscribe, but I manage to see most of the shows. *The Importance of Being Earnest* was most enjoyable and I'm looking forward to *Sleuth*."

"Thanks," she replied. "It's always nice to meet a fan."

"Now, I have to lock up, but I'd like to continue this chat." Father More took her arm. "Would you care to come to the rectory? It's right next door and I can make us a cup of tea."

"That sounds nice," she said, glancing at her watch, "but I don't want to miss the last bus."

"Oh, dear, I'm afraid you already have. I saw it go by a moment ago. But I will run you home in my car. Where do you live?"

"Chestnut Street. It's not far, I can walk."

"It's cold and dark, and I'd feel better knowing you have a ride."

"All right, you convinced me." She and Benton walked most places together, but a ride on a cold night was always welcome.

"Now, shall we go next door?" He locked the sanctuary door and led the way.

The rectory was a Victorian building, complementing the architecture of the cathedral. Inside, the oak-paneled walls gleamed with polish. Father More led the way past two sitting rooms, through the dining room—an elegant chamber with a long table seating twelve—to the homey kitchen at the back of the house.

He put the kettle on the stove and opened a large tin. "Oh, good—shortbread." He put a few on a plate. "Our housekeeper is a wonderful cook."

When the water boiled, he handed a mug to Deirdre and carrying the cookies and his own tea, led the way to one of the sitting rooms. "This is my personal study. Make yourself comfortable."

A poster from the movie *The Lord of the Rings* hung next to two framed diplomas. Deirdre noticed he had an MA in English Literature as well as a master of divinity and smiled at the interesting combination. She walked around the room perusing the many bookcases. From Bible commentaries and Sunday school curriculum, she moved on to shelves of fiction. She expected to find books by J.R.R. Tolkien and C.S. Lewis, but she was surprised at the horror stories that seemed to make up the majority of his collection. He had classics like *Dracula, Frankenstein,* and *Doctor Jekyll and Mr. Hyde; 'Salem's Lot* and a shelf of books by Stephen King; and *Interview with the Vampire* headed the row of Vampire Chronicles by Anne Rice. She ran her fingers over other titles.

Father More sat down near the fireplace. "I see you have discovered my passion for gothic literature. It keeps me aware of how close the dark side is to the light. Demons masquerade in many garments."

Deirdre pulled out his copy of *The Vampire Book: The Encyclopedia of the Undead.* "You seem to like vampires." She leafed through the hefty volume, glancing at some of the pictures.

"Yes, I do. I could regale you for hours with ways to recognize them—cold hands, pale skin, prominent teeth, alluring and sometimes hypnotic eyes—ways to test for their presence, like offering garlic—and, of course, ways to destroy them. The lore behind them is fascinating—I see you found my *Vampire Book*—and I like the struggle between good and evil. It's more clear-cut than some zombie movies for example. I didn't enjoy *Night of the Living Dead*."

"I never thought a priest would watch zombie movies." Deirdre chuckled as she picked up her mug of tea and sat down.

"Well, as I said, it's a hobby. And it's one way I keep abreast of popular culture." He passed her the cookies. "Now, tell me about yourself. You said you worked at the theater, are you an actress?

"No, one of the crew. This season has kept us pretty busy so far. At least *Sleuth* is modern dress—that will be a nice break."

"I take it you work with the costumes?"

"I'm the wardrobe mistress—I clean and repair the costumes used in the current production, help the actors with changes, stuff like that."

"It sounds interesting." He sipped his tea.

"I love it—it's a job, but it's fun, not like real work to me. Well, once in a while there's an obnoxious actor, but most of them are nice."

She reached for a piece of shortbread. "It keeps me busy. I don't know many people in town. In fact, I only just met my neighbor—he works nights, too."

"I imagine your hours make it hard to meet people. I know they have performances on holidays. I'm glad I took the chance to get to know you tonight." He pointed to her empty mug. "Can I get you some more tea?"

She shook her head. "No, thanks. I should be getting home. I may be used to late hours, but I don't want to impose."

"Let me find my keys and we'll be off. We'll have to do this again sometime." He helped her with her coat.

"Thank you, Father. I'd like that."

FOUR

A few weeks passed by. One show closed and after the hectic week of set put-in, light hanging and final dress rehearsals, the next one opened. The routine of the new production settled, and Deirdre realized she hadn't seen Benton for a while.

One night she decided to short-cut through the old graveyard. An odd choice for a late night ramble, but it always seemed to be deserted, even during the day. Deirdre had come through there several times with Benton and grown fond of the solitary route. A gibbous moon hung in the cloudless sky that night, its hunched back shedding a faint silver glimmer on the tree-lined paths between the tombstones.

She didn't need the moon to see the inscriptions — she knew her favorite ones by heart. She let her hand brush over the chiseled letters, reading the words with her fingers:

Stranger pause as you pass by

As you are now so once was I
As I am now so you will be
Stop and say a prayer for me.

She passed beneath the permanently outspread wings of a stone angel and felt a whispered tear:

God's finger touched him and he slept.

Then the one that left her with the ineffective sorrow of a life cut off too soon:

Precious darling, thou hast left us,
left us yes, forever more.
But we hope to meet our loved one
on that right and happy shore.

A cold breeze rattled the branches as she hurried along and she was thankful to shave a few minutes off the walk home. Her footsteps crunched on the frozen gravel and an owl whooed from his perch above a mausoleum.

Something caught her eye—maybe a trick of the evanescent moonlight—and she peered over a grave marker. Had she seen movement? The shifting pattern of the moon shadows made it hard to tell.

She heard a sound like a low moan. *Maybe that's the owl again.*

"Is someone there?" she called.

"Is that Deirdre?" A crouching figure detached from the jagged shadow of a nearby tree. "It's me, Benton."

Now she could make him out, kneeling next to someone on the ground. "What are you doing? Is something wrong?"

"It's not what you think, Deirdre."

"How could you possibly know what I think?"

He stood up. "I mean—I'm not gay."

"I didn't think you were gay, Ben. To be honest, I thought you were a vampire." She gasped and clapped her hand over her mouth. She hadn't meant to voice this hatching idea without consideration.

He drew in a rasping breath, and as his mouth opened she saw, for the first time, a glimpse of his long, sharpened eyeteeth. "How did you know?"

"I put together a few clues. You even said you were one of the children of the night. But in my heart I wondered if I was being silly—making a shot in the dark."

"Very perceptive. It was straight in the gold." He put his hand, trembling, on her shoulder. "Are you a slayer? On a 'the only good vampire is a dead vampire' crusade?"

A slayer? She looked at him. "I thought all vampires *were* dead."

"Touché." He sighed. "So, what are you going to do about me?"

"Do I have to do something? You're the first vampire I ever met and I happen to like you. That's a

35

bit of a problem. I think I'll hold off judgment a while before I sharpen a stake."

"Thanks. I'll try to be worthy of your faith." He took her hand. "Come on, I'll walk you home."

As they turned away, this time she knew she heard a moan. "Ben, there's someone there."

He hustled her toward the path. "He'll be okay. He'll sleep for a while. It's just a temporary weakness."

"One of your . . . victims?" she wondered.

He nodded.

She stopped, her fists planted on her hips. "We can't just leave him there—it's too cold. He could die of exposure."

"What do you want me to do?" he asked, spreading his hands.

"Call the police. You have a cell phone."

"And tell them what?"

She shrugged. "Personally, I'd tell them the truth."

"And that would be—what? You were walking in the graveyard when you ran into a vampire?" A cynical note edged his voice.

"Not entirely—you have to be clever." She rubbed her forehead. "Look, there's a police car at the corner—I'll talk to him."

He grabbed her sleeve. "Deirdre, you can't."

"Do you trust me?" she asked.

"Do I have a choice?" he retorted.

"Not really. Now hide. And watch me." She pulled out of his grip and ran to the gate.

The officer in the car saw her running and climbed out of the cruiser. "Can I help you, young lady?"

"I'm fine, but there's a man back there who's ill." She pointed over her shoulder. "He needs a hospital or something."

He signaled to his partner. "Show us the place."

She led the policemen back to the graveyard.

The first officer pulled out a notebook. "Can you tell us what happened?"

"I don't really know anything. I was walking home from work—I work at the Union Square Theater— when I almost tripped over this man lying on the ground. I think he's alive—I heard him moan." She crossed her arms, trying to disguise a nervous shiver.

"Do you know him?" The officer scribbled on his pad.

Deirdre shook her head. "Oh, no, I never saw him before."

He looked up. "Do you always walk home alone?"

"Yes. I'm one of the last to leave the theater."

"We'll take it from here, miss." He put the notebook in his pocket. "Thanks for your cooperation. I just need your name and address in case we have to get in touch."

She filled out the form they gave her and sighed with relief as they bundled the unfortunate gentleman into the car and drove away.

"The truth." Ben emerged from behind a bush and took her arm, chuckling, as they headed home.

She shrugged. "They should have asked if I saw anybody else."

"Thank you for not giving me away."

"You're welcome."

They walked in silence for a few minutes.

"I wish . . ." Ben began, then groaned. "Oh, God, I wish it didn't have to be like this."

"That you weren't a vampire?" she asked.

"Every day for over one hundred and forty years I've made that wish."

"How did it happen?"

"I suppose you deserve to know." Ben did not meet Deirdre's eyes as he told her the story. "It was during the War of Secession. I had to enlist. The North was inflicting their values on our lives—with aggression. Taking a stand against them was the patriotic thing to do . . ."

* * * *

My mother brushed a thread from the shoulder of my new gray coat. "There you are, Benton. My, don't you look handsome." She adjusted my belt.

I held her hands to stop the fiddling. "Mother, are you sure you want me to go? I could stay to run the plantation for you. The army will understand."

"Don't be silly, dear. Besides, it's not a plantation any more—it's just a farm now. Your Uncle Jack said he'll help us out. Don't worry about a thing. We're going to be just fine. Your father and brother have been gone for a year—it's your turn now. Make me proud." She dabbed her eyes and tucked the hanky in her sleeve.

I stiffened my shoulders. "Very well. I'll do my best."

"I want you to have this." She gave me a little silken bag. "It was my grandmother's, so it's been well prayed over."

I peered into the bag at the worn wooden beads of her rosary, then tucked the treasure into my breast pocket. "Thank you, Mother. I'll always keep it near my heart."

She handed me my hat. "Now, before you leave, there's a photographer in town this week. I want a picture."

"Oh, Mother."

"Humor me, Benton. The others did." Their framed portraits sat in a place of honor on the piano. "I need something to remember my boy."

"How can I refuse?" I kissed her smooth cheek.

There was glory in marching to war. At the farewell Gala, the older women made sure the soldiers danced with every pretty girl. The town turned out to cheer the latest recruits. My spirit soared with pride as we paraded past the bright new flag. I grinned at the men beside me. There was camaraderie around the campfires as we pitched our tents for the night. Our talk rang with hope as we spoke of routing the Yankees and sending them home.

There was glory in marching to war. There was little glory in war.

I wasn't bred to be a soldier. I knew how to handle a gun—I'd been hunting since I could keep up with my father in the woods—but I didn't know how to fight. You don't learn what that's like on a training ground.

Under relentless noise—gunfire, cannon fire, screams of wounded men, and far above it all the shriek of carrion birds—we tried to shoot. Load-aim-fire . . . load-aim-fire. That I could do as long as I did not think too hard on whether my bullets found their marks. I was a good shot. They probably did.

Nobody can teach you what it's like to stand at the edge of a victor's battlefield and see strewn across it from end to end the hunched piles of corpse-filled clothing that are all that remains of brothers . . . comrades . . . enemies.

Those nights I lay with my guts torn and aching from retching and my pillow soaked with tears wondering if it was worth waking up in the morning to face another battle or another march.

We marched until boots cracked and feet bled. When I wore the soles of my boots to shreds, I marched barefoot. No one had new footgear unless you could scavenge them off a dead man. Our smart new uniforms faded, and we wore what was whole regardless of color. Shiny brass buttons, lost or bartered for food, we replaced with sliced twigs, shaped and polished with our pocketknives.

A cannonGala that tore my friend's head from his shoulders ripped what courage I thought I had from my heart. Lying on the ground using his mutilated corpse as a shield, I forced my shaking fingers to load my rifle, but they couldn't manage the familiar motions. I rolled over and stared up at a sky as leaden as the bullet in my hand.

Dear God, where are you in this? Where is the end? I wiped blood, brains and bone chips off my face with my sleeve and let my hand drop to my chest. I felt the little bag with the rosary and took some comfort in the fact that my mother prayed for me. I lived to march to another battle.

Battle? It seemed like an excursion into the netherworld. Sweat that poured into my eyes and mosquitoes that sang in my ears and stabbed at my neck multiplied my discomfort. A swinging branch whipped my eye. It soon swelled shut. The tepid water in my bottle did nothing to quench my thirst.

By the end of the day, my ears rang with constant gunfire and I fought dizziness with every step. Then suddenly, a hell-like fire exploded under my arm and for me the battle was over. Sounds muted to a distant roar—no gunfire, no screams, no birds, and no running brook. Sight faded like a sun-washed photograph.

A weight pressed on my chest; I wanted to breathe, but shards of pain lanced my lungs with every effort. I knew I was dying. Someone held me, bathed my face and dribbled watered brandy in my mouth.

"I'm scared," I gasped, "I don't want to die."

"I can help, if you trust me." He looked into my eyes. "No more suffering—no more dying. You won't ever hurt again."

He touched my chest, and the weight seemed to ease. He lifted his hand, red with my blood, and licked his fingers.

"Please," I whispered, "just take the pain away." My vision dimmed as he bent over me, pressing his mouth to my wound.

When I woke, he was lying next to me, smiling. I groped inside my shirt, but my fingers met only smooth, whole skin. I touched my eye; the swelling was gone. If not for the holes in my bloodstained shirt, I might have thought it was a dream. But what was the dream? The battle or the healing?

"You're like me now," he said, "all this—" he waved his hand in the moonlight and I saw men around us dead and dying "—is a banquet. Come, let us feed ..."

* * * *

"The making of a vampire." Benton looked at Deirdre now. "That is how I came to be what I am today."

"After all the brutality, it must have been horrible—in pain and dying, I can see how you might have grasped at any way out."

"Don't think I haven't thought the same thing as I try to justify my life. Did I deserve to live? Would death—that clean and honest death—have been so bad? I used to think about heaven before—I could have chosen heaven—but I sold out to my pain."

She took his cold hand and linked her fingers through his. "I wouldn't have met you if you hadn't. I guess that sounds a little selfish."

Something flickered through his eyes—hope or pain—Deirdre wasn't sure which.

"No," Benton stared at their intertwined hands. "I'm glad we met. But that choice weighs on me like a curse I can never break."

"Isn't there any way for you to change?"

"If there were, Deirdre, I'd take it in a second. The others laugh at me—a vampire turning down immortality—but they don't have any hope to offer. They don't want any hope."

"There must be something. Where there's life, there is hope."

He made a bitter sound. "No life, remember, I'm undead."

"Well, maybe you don't have life, but I do, Benton. Let me think about things."

"I could hardly stop you. No one else has ever cared to try." He put his arms lightly around her.

She hugged him, her head pressed against his chest. "Good night for now. I'll see you tomorrow."

"Good night."

FIVE

A knock roused Deirdre early the next morning. She squinted at the glare of sunlight battling her curtains and fumbled for the clock. "Who's there?" she called.

"Lieutenant Bowen, Miss Maguire. I'm with the police. I hate to bother you so early, but I'd like to have a few words with you."

Police? How could she refuse? She sighed, expecting they would want to talk about last night. "Could you wait a minute while I get dressed?"

"Certainly."

Deirdre sprinted for the bathroom. Cold water and clean teeth helped her face the unexpectedly early day. She grabbed a pair of blue jeans and a turtleneck sweater. Her shoes, as usual, had migrated under the bed. She fished them out, ran a brush through her hair, and opened the door.

"Good morning. Is it—Lieutenant?"

"Yes, miss. Lieutenant Bowen."

"Come in. Would you like some coffee? I'm just going to start a pot." She filled the carafe, added coffee, and shoved some bread in the toaster.

"Thanks, I'd like a cup." He pulled out a chair and sat at the table. "If you don't mind, Cummings here will take notes." The officer joined them at the table.

She filled mugs and set out milk and sugar. When the toast popped up, she slathered on butter and hoped a sip of the hot brew would steady her racing heart.

"How can I help you?" she asked.

"I understand you reported an injured man in the park last night."

"That's right."

Lieutenant Bowen flipped a page in his notebook. "Did you notice any wounds on the body?"

"Well, I didn't get close enough to touch him," she said. "I could hear him moan, so I knew he was alive."

"You didn't get close, yet you say he was a man?" The lieutenant made it a question.

"To be accurate—from where I stood, the person appeared to be dressed in male clothing, so I assumed he was a man. The officers who picked him up confirmed that."

"Thank you, Miss Maguire. It's always important to be accurate. Did you notice anyone else in the area?"

Uh-oh. She knew Lieutenant Bowen would see right through an evasion. In order not to cast a bad light on Benton, she thought her words through carefully before she spoke, then took a deep breath. "Yes I did."

Lieutenant Bowen tapped his notebook and waited. "Go on."

"It was Benton Colyer. He's a friend of mine. In fact, he lives across the hall here."

"I've heard the name." He thought a moment. "A DJ, isn't he? With a late night program, I believe."

She let out the rest of the breath. "Yes, that's right."

"What was Mr. Colyer doing?"

"I didn't ask."

"Weren't you surprised to see him?" Lieutenant Bowman asked.

Deirdre shook her head. "Not really. I just assumed he was walking home, the same as me."

"Do you happen to remember the time?"

She frowned, thinking. "It must have been shortly after midnight. I don't normally see Ben unless I stop at the studio. He's usually there until two. Didn't the officer put down the time in his report?"

"Oh, yes, he did. I just wanted to double check." He turned another page. "Do you meet Mr. Colyer often?"

"Occasionally. As I said, we're friends."

"After midnight?"

"That's our usual time." She shrugged. "We both work at night."

"What about Tuesday?"

Deirdre closed her eyes as she thought back. "Tuesday. Okay, I remember. I did go to the studio. You can check with the night guard—he logs in all the visitors. We stopped at a café for something to eat, and then we walked home."

"Is that a normal activity for the two of you?"

"Yes." She grinned. "We're night owls."

"All right. Do you remember the time that night?"

"I suppose it must have been about three when we left the café. Somebody there might remember. Why do you ask?" She suddenly felt cold. "Did something happen?"

"Hmm." He snapped his notebook shut. "There was a similar incident that night about one o'clock. If the alibi checks out, neither of you could have been involved. I appreciate your help."

"Anytime, Lieutenant."

She breathed a sigh of relief as he closed the door, but the sliver of cold dread still lingered. *A similar incident?* She shivered, wondering what that could mean. "I'll have to tell Ben."

The day dragged on to noon. She let a pot of vegetable beef soup simmer for a while and mixed a batch of whole wheat biscuits. While they were baking, she knocked on Ben's door. "I made some soup; will you come have lunch with me?"

"No, I won't." His answer sounded firm. "Deirdre, a vampire can't enter your home unless you invite him in."

"I know that. It's okay. I *am* inviting you in. I trust you."

"You shouldn't. You don't understand what it means."

She leaned her head against his door. "This is important, Ben. I need to talk to you now. I don't want to wait until after work."

"All right, I'll come." He hesitated at her door for a bit as she set the table, then crossed the room and sat down. "What's so important?"

"The police were here."

"About last night?"

"Yes. And about Tuesday. Apparently there was a 'similar situation.' I know it wasn't you, Ben. But you said something about 'the others.' Are there other vampires?"

He sighed. "Oh, yes. A few, not as many as some more populous cities, but they are here, and they have an Enclave beneath the old Athenaeum building."

She stared at him. "The Athenaeum? But that's where the theater is."

"I know." He fidgeted with his spoon.

"The lower level has a night club and the kitchens for the restaurant are down there, too. It's busy all the time. Wouldn't people notice a bunch of vampires?"

"There are levels beneath the kitchens that few people know about, plumbing and ductwork that are no longer used. It's enough for them." He looked up into her face. "Don't worry, if I thought you were in danger, I'd haunt the place—I could do it quite effectively, too." He grinned, teeth glinting.

The thought sent a shiver up her spine. "But *you* don't go there?"

He shook his head. "No, we had a falling out. You see, they like being vampires. And then there was Sidell . . ."

"Sidell? He followed me one night."

"That's not surprising. He's the only vampire I ever made. I didn't want to, but in the end I didn't have much choice. It was in another city—but cities are so much the same—and another time, but after all these years, even times seem much the same. Work was hard to find then; war in Europe was brewing. One night I was hunting and I met him near the train station—always a good place to find a victim even in bad weather—and that night a thin sleet froze the streets . . .

* * * *

The young man turned up his collar as he huddled under the shelter by the tracks. The shoulders of his jacket were dark with rain, and his pale hair was plastered to his brow. "Take me home with you? Please?"

It was a bad night to ply that trade. He hadn't been on the streets long—he was plump, and his good quality clothes were still clean. I knew where he could sell them for a meal and a bed. They'd be gone before Sunday if no one helped him out.

"Come here." I didn't want to help him—I just wanted to feed—but I felt him shiver at my touch. I knew that if I fed and left him asleep in the cold, he wouldn't last the night. I preferred not to get involved with my victims, but some lingering shred of humanity kept me from leaving him to die. "You can stay with me tonight."

"Thank you," he gasped.

I strode ahead, not caring if he kept up, but he managed to stay at my heels. I let him in to my apartment and gave him brandy to stir his blood.

"Your clothes are nice. Why don't you have an overcoat? Or a place to live for that matter?"

"My father threw me out." The glass rattled against his chattering teeth until he managed to swallow some of the brandy. "I sold my coat three days ago."

"How old are you? You can't be twenty." His plump body and smooth, fair skin made him seem more a boy than a grown man to me.

"Eighteen." He shrugged, looking like a bedraggled peacock as he draped his wet clothing over a chair.

I drew him a bath and found a clean nightshirt. "No job?"

"I'll find something." He held out the empty glass for more brandy.

While he bathed, I prepared for the night—my only thought of the feeding that was to come. I didn't want a meal, so I fixed none for him. He had another brandy, and reeled drunkenly to my bed.

I had no desire to lie with him, but he seemed to expect it, and held his arms out to me like a child. I stretched out beside him, looking into his eyes until his eyelids fluttered and fell shut. Then I drank deeply from his veins and fell asleep myself. It was near evening when we finally awoke.

"Don't get up," he said as I moved, "I don't know what you did last night, but between the way it made me feel and the dreams I had, it was better than opium."

He hadn't used any for days—I would have tasted it in his blood. "Are you an addict? Is that why your father threw you out?"

He hung his head. "He said I wasted his money. He wouldn't even try some for himself."

"And so now you whore for a living?"

"Why not? I used to do it for the drugs, but now . . ." A strange smile twisted his mouth. "At least I have *those* skills."

"It's time for you to go," I answered, suddenly out of patience with him.

He pulled on his clothes. "All right, but we will meet again, won't we? I'd like it."

"Perhaps," I said, but I had no plans to seek him out.

He paused at the door. "Well, in that case, my name's Sidell Prentis."

I told him my name and he left.

I met him about a month later near a club in the old vaudeville district.

"Benton, hello. I've been hoping I would see you again." He spread his arms. "How lucky we should run into each other."

I stopped, surprised he remembered. "Sidell. You seem happy. Have you found work, a place to stay?"

He still looked well fed, and he had acquired an overcoat, but underneath, his fancy clothes showed signs of wear.

"Of course—I can always find someone who'll pay for my services." He stepped close enough to whisper in my ear. "Could we get together? Like last time?"

My mouth watered at the thought. "Why not?" I'd never had a willing victim before.

We met again about two weeks after that. In my enjoyment of the moment, I hardly thought to wonder at the coincidence. When I ran into him again after a week, it was obvious he had been stalking me. Our rendezvous became more numerous, and one early morning I came home and found he had moved his belongings into my apartment.

"What have you done? You can't stay here!"

"Why not?" he asked. "I sleep here almost every day as it is."

Had our encounters grown that frequent? After a minute's thought, my anger faded as I realized that they had. His eagerness made his blood taste sweeter, and I was as drawn to him, as he seemed to be attracted to me.

Some times he'd stay out all night; I could smell the drugs or liquor he'd been using and I never fed on him then. His stay stretched from days to weeks—he seemed to depend on me or perhaps on my need for him—and I satisfied my blood lust by taking blatant advantage of him.

One day while we dressed, he stood buttoning his shirt and admiring himself in the mirror. "All my life

I've been fat. I never knew how nice it is to be slim until now."

I remembered his body had been plump and soft, now he was thin to the point of frailty.

"I wonder if I'm a little too pale?" He leaned forward, smoothing his sleek blond hair. "No . . . no . . . not really. I've always been fair skinned, and we do tend to live out our lives at night." He smiled at his reflection. "I think I look terribly elegant. What do you think, Benton?"

He had not lost any of his good looks, but now I saw an ashy pallor underlying his normally light complexion and I noticed he sometimes gasped as if unable to catch his breath. How could I have been so blind not to see his condition declining? I knew I should not have fed so much from one person, but he made it hard to resist. If I didn't stop soon he would die. Even now it might be too late.

"Sid." As I touched his shoulder wondering what I could say to apologize, I felt a familiar pang at seeing only his reflection in the mirror.

He adjusted his tie and turned, stroking his neck where the red marks of the wounds I made showed vivid on his blanched skin. "I know what you are, Benton, I know what you've been doing to me," he said, smiling. "I've never felt this exhilaration before—at least not from drugs. Trust me, I've tried. I want more—I want it for myself." His shadowed eyes gleamed hard as stones. "Make me like you."

I swallowed but my mouth was dry. "No, Sid. I can't."

"You mean you won't. Please, Benton. I'm begging you."

"I won't inflict this torment on another person."

"You don't want to share your immortality," he complained. "You call it torment because you don't want anyone else to know what heaven is like."

"It isn't heaven to me—it's hell. Don't make me do it."

"Well, then, tonight—will you feed?"

"No, Sid. I'm afraid for you. If I take more blood, you'll fall ill." I couldn't bring myself to say die.

"Don't be silly. I've never been sick before." He pouted. "Tomorrow night, then?"

"We'll see."

There is an Enclave of vampires in every city. They are the ones who seek to increase our numbers. I hated being part of them. I still do. Sid sought them out. I don't know how he found them—they usually hide from mortals. Perhaps the blood-bond that was forging between us attuned Sid to their presence. One day they sent a summons I could not ignore.

I stood in the Vault and confronted the Eldest, a vampire so ancient we no longer remembered his name. "You know I don't need to be part of this. If you want him—you make him."

He refused. "I can't, it's gone too far. You've marked him as your own. *You* must do it; if I bite him, he'll die—look at him, Benton, he's dying anyway."

Whether I liked it or not, I had to admit that was true.

"He asked to be made." The Eldest ordered, "Make him, Benton, or I'll see you in hell."

I groaned, "I am *already* in hell."

They carried Sidell in on a cot. In the few days since I had seen him last his health had deteriorated dramatically—he was now too weak to stand. His hollow eyes burned with fever and he struggled to draw every rasping breath.

The Eldest nodded as I looked at him. "There isn't much time."

I sat on the bed and looked into his eyes, my tears falling on his wasted face, but my dying friend smiled. "Dear Benton. Don't be sorry. You haven't wronged me. I want you to make me a vampire— more than anything. It's a dream come true."

He put his arms around my neck and pulled my head toward his throat, moaning with delight as my teeth sank into his neck. I drank his blood until he lay drained and unconscious in my arms, then wiped my mouth on my sleeve.

Someone pressed a silver knife into my outstretched hand. I drew it across my wrist, opening the vein, letting my blood trickle onto Sidell's lips. When his eyes finally flickered and he licked the blood, I pressed the wound to his mouth. I could feel his strength return as my blood flowed into him. I let him drink until my vision grew dark and I fainted.

I woke in my own room, alone and weeping for the soul I had condemned to hell. The wound on my arm was already merely a fading red line. I cursed the day

I became this monster and I swore I would never make another vampire . . .

****

Benton wiped his face with the back of his hand. "If there was anything I could do to break this devil's curse, I would do it. Let me go, Deirdre. You're foolish to even talk to me. You only put yourself in danger." He pushed aside his uneaten food and ran out of her studio.

When she knocked at his door before she went to work that night, he didn't answer.

SIX

Deirdre discovered she enjoyed exploring the strange world of the night. She grew to love the dark and glittering city with its sometimes queer and alluring businesses. She had known the discount chain store was always open and the nightclub in the Athenaeum served the after-theater crowd, but that had been the extent of her late-night knowledge. Ben introduced her to restaurants, a bookstore, a boutique specializing in vintage clothes and even found an all-night dry cleaner that gave her a discount for items delivered after midnight.

As she spent more time with Ben, she began to adjust herself to his sleep patterns. She stayed at the theater after the show ended to make repairs or start the laundry and Ben would meet her there. Often they stayed out until four or five in the morning, but she could always make up by sleeping until noon.

One day after the Sunday matinee, she sat at her desk doodling as she ate a sandwich. She drew a line down the page and headed one side What I Like About Ben. Quickly she filled in his positive attributes: handsome, intelligent, good job, fun to be with . . .

She paused, wondering if it was shallow to put his appearance before his brains. She added polite and good sense of humor, then scratched out the last entry. She hadn't seen much evidence of humor, except a wry twist to his words now and then. But under the circumstances, what did she expect?

She tapped her eraser on the other column. It had no heading yet. She didn't want to write What I Don't Like About Ben. If she wrote those words, she'd have to admit that one thing she didn't like. *He is a vampire. How much did that make him into this person I like so much?* She thought of some more words for the pro side: adaptable, resourceful. She ripped the paper into shreds and crumpled them into the garbage.

She'd never met anyone like Benton before, and there was more to him than the short list she had written. He moved her, and she liked the way that made her feel. What would it mean have a relationship with a vampire? What would that relationship look like?

She knew she was falling in love with him, and what's more she enjoyed every minute of the experience. Maybe she could ignore that dark part of him? No. Maybe she could find someone to talk to — someone who might believe the improbable story.

She checked the clock—it was almost time for evening mass. She hadn't seen Ben since yesterday, maybe he'd enjoy going with her. She knocked at his door.

"Who is it?"

"It's Deirdre. I'm going out for a while, will you come with me?" She leaned against the wall in the hallway.

"I told you not to see me anymore. I'll hurt you."

"You might. But I think it's worth the chance." She knocked again. "Ben, just come with me, okay?"

He opened the door. "Worth the chance? Do you know what you're saying?"

"I think so." She reached out for his hand. "And I want to help if I can."

He sighed. "All right. I'll get my coat."

He came out a moment later pulling his hat down over his eyes. She took his hand, and his strong fingers felt icy. He took her arm as they left the building, and they walked in quiet companionship. She led him to the church; welcoming light spilled out the door as people arrived for the service.

"Oh. Church. I can't go in there," he said.

The massive front of the gray stone cathedral could appear forbidding to someone unfamiliar. "It's okay. You don't have to be Catholic to attend a service."

"It's not that, in fact I *am* Catholic—at least I was brought up that way. No . . . I can't get in. The door is barred to me."

People opened and shut the door, laughing and chatting as they gathered, moving freely through the portico. Deirdre watched. "I don't understand."

"Maybe this will explain." He put his finger on the silver cross that hung against her throat. She felt only the cool pressure of his finger, but he held it there, grimacing as if with pain. When he showed her the finger it had been seared and blistered, branded with the shape of the pendant. "I would burn like this if I stepped inside," he said.

She cradled his hand in hers. "That hurts."

"Oh, yes. Here—" he held out his finger "—and here." He tapped his chest, the burn rapidly fading. "My body heals, that is one of the *blessings* of my damned condition, but some hurts are not so easily healed. I am cursed—I can never come to a place of God again. Enjoy yourself, Deirdre. I'll see you later." He strode off, his black clothes swept around him, blending him into the shadows.

She sat through Mass that night, following the service, saying the right words at the appropriate times, but her mind could not focus on worship. She gazed at the stained glass window near her pew, glowing in the night from the outside light. Russell Wheelock had donated an illustration of the Prodigal Son

"So, Russell," she thought, "what kind of man were you? Were you the prodigal too? Or maybe you were the father. Would you have chosen this picture if the story hadn't touched your heart?"

"That's one of the loveliest windows in the sanctuary."

Deirdre jumped. "Hi, Father More. I guess I was letting my mind wander again."

The priest grinned. "I didn't mean to startle you, but you did seem a bit preoccupied."

"Well, yes. I was thinking about that story." She pointed to the window.

"The Prodigal Son? One of my favorites. I played a bit of a prodigal myself at one time. It's good to know that no matter what we do, the Father will welcome us back."

"He wants all of us back, doesn't he—no matter what we've done?"

"Indeed he does."

"Even if you lived under a devil's curse?"

"Ahh . . . yes, I believe so." Father More nodded. "After all, even Mina Harker was redeemed in the end."

"M-mina Harker?" Deirdre felt a jolt at such an appropriate reference.

"From the story *Dracula*, by Bram Stoker. Forgive me; perhaps you're not familiar with the book."

"On the contrary, I've read it."

He took her arm. "But you look distressed, my child, I hope it's nothing I said?"

"No—or rather, yes." Deirdre shivered. "That reference to vampires hits a little close to home."

"How intriguing." He paused. "Perhaps if you could be a little more specific, I could be of more assistance."

"I'd like to, but it is not my story."

He nodded with understanding.

She continued. "Just tell me one thing, Father. Do you believe vampires exist?"

"I have no proof they do not exist, so, yes, I have to say I do," he said. "The literature is quite compelling."

Deirdre looked up, pleading with her eyes. "Then would it be true that a vampire can be redeemed?"

He nodded slowly. "As I said, Mina Harker was restored, although she had not completely turned. But of course, for redemption, he—or she—must truly desire transformation."

Deirdre felt relief and a glimmer of hope for Benton. "Well, thank you, that's what I wondered. I think I've kept you late enough. I have to go. Good night, Father."

"Good night. If there is anything else I can do, anything you'd like to tell me, be assured it will stay private with me."

"Thank you, I'll remember that." She raised her hand to wave as the door closed behind her.

SEVEN

Rhonda called to Deirdre from the box office window. "Come here, I have something fabulous to tell you."

Deirdre leaned closer. "Oh, please tell."

"I went to the nightclub downstairs after work the other night, and I saw the cutest guy. You know, the kind with blond hair and blue eyes that makes you say, Wow? Then he actually came over to talk to me! I could not believe it." She fanned herself with her hand. "And to top it off, he says he knows you and he's an old friend of Benton Colyer, too."

"Not Sidell Prentis?" Somehow Deirdre knew it would be.

"Yes, that's him. We've been out every night this week. Isn't he absolutely adorable?" She sighed with apparent delight.

"That's not how I would describe him, although he is good looking." Deirdre reached under the glass to take her hand. "Look, Rhonda, I don't think you should go out with him."

Rhonda pushed the hand away. "Hold it, Deirdre, you don't get every cute guy who comes along. This one is mine."

"Don't worry, I don't want him." Deirdre frowned. "I just think he's . . . dangerous."

"Ooh . . . dangerous . . . now that sounds exciting." Rhonda's eyes lit up.

"Please. I know you don't want a warning." Deirdre gave one anyway. "Just be careful."

"I will. But why are you being so negative? This time I didn't I pick up a total stranger like you always yell at me for. Sidell's a friend of yours for heaven's sake. Besides, I thought it would be fun. Me and Sid — you and Benton — we can double date." She flicked her hair over her shoulder. "He's picking me up after work, you and Benton can meet us later. What do you think?"

Deirdre sighed. "I don't know. I'll have to check with Ben."

"Okay, suit yourselves. I can't say I mind having Sid all to myself for the night."

"Watch out, Rhonda. Don't let him go too far."

"Right. What fun is that?" She frowned. "I don't see the harm in having a little fling. I'm not exactly a nun, you know."

"Yeah, I know." Deirdre slung her bag over her shoulder and headed backstage. She needed to talk to Ben, but it would have to wait until the show was over.

Later that evening, Deirdre greeted the radio station security guard. He never asked for her ID anymore—just filled in her name on the clipboard. She walked quietly down the hall and looked in the studio window. Ben waved, pointed to his watch and held up five fingers. She nodded and headed for the kitchenette to get some coffee. Benton would join her when the news came on in five minutes. She grinned to herself at how familiar she had become with the routine.

"How is everything with you this fine night?" Ben opened the refrigerator and took out a pitcher of filtered water.

"I'm okay, but I'm worried about Rhonda. She's hooked up with Sidell."

"That's not good." Water slopped on the counter as his hand shook and he set the jug down. "This is my fault. They've sent him to bring me back to the Enclave. They wouldn't hesitate at using you and Rhonda to get to me."

"What can we do? I tried to warn her, but she didn't want to listen." She pulled out a chair at the small café table.

He swallowed some water. "I may have to go back. Try as I might, it gets harder all the time for me to keep away."

"Oh, no, Ben. You shouldn't have to do that." Not when she had hopes he could change.

"I won't put you and Rhonda in danger. They would like nothing better than to draw you into their

67

world. I'm already one of them—what more can they do to me?"

"It's asking too much." She sprinkled creamer in her coffee.

"I'm part of that world whether I like it or not—it's one of the consequences I have to bear." He checked the wall clock. "I have some work to do on the program for tomorrow. It shouldn't take more than an hour. Wait for me and we'll find them when I'm done."

They didn't have to look farther than Luigi's, the restaurant where Ben had taken Deirdre on their first night out. Sid and Rhonda had a cozy table and it seemed that they had just eaten their meal—the dirty dishes were pushed aside as they finished a bottle of Chianti.

Sid nudged Rhonda. "Well, well. Look who's here."

Deirdre pulled out a chair across from them.

"You don't mind if we join you, do you?" Ben sat next to her.

"It seems you already have." Sid smiled. "But we're always glad to have you."

The waiter cleared the plates and offered dessert. Deirdre asked for espresso.

Ben leaned across the table. "What do you want, Sidell?"

"Everybody asks me that! What makes you think I want something?" He widened his clear blue eyes with a seemingly innocent look.

"I know you, Sid. As a matter of fact, I think you want *me*." Ben glared. "Did the Eldest send you?"

Rhonda looked from one to the other. "What are you boys talking about? Which eldest? You have to tell me everything." She plopped her elbows on the table and leaned forward.

"Never mind, Rhonda. This is business between me and Benton." Sid crossed his arms. "You must think a lot of yourself, Benton. Why would we want you? An old man, wasting away his life. We want *them*—fresh new blood, young pretty girls."

"Old man?" Rhonda stifled a yelp as Deirdre kicked her ankle. She whispered across the table at her friend. "Why does this eldest want us? It's not some porn thing, is it?"

"No—don't be silly. Now hush. Listen. You might learn something." Deirdre sipped her coffee. She wanted to take Ben's hand, but he held them clenched on the table.

"Don't bring the girls down, Sid. I know Deirdre doesn't want that"

Sid tipped his head to one side. "Do you *know* that? I think you care about Deirdre, at any rate I suspect she cares about you. What do you whisper to her in the small, dark hours? Do you tell her of eternity?" He drew Rhonda close to him and breathed "Eternity" in her ear. She giggled as he lightly kissed her neck, her cheek, and then her lips.

Rhonda sighed, smiling. "I've never met anyone like Sid before. He makes me feel special." She drew her chair closer, snuggling next to him and laying her head on his shoulder.

Sid stroked Rhonda's hair. "Look at Deirdre, Benton. She looks so soft and warm. Just like Rhonda. Do you sleep with her?"

"No." Ben jerked his hand, tipping his coffee, and spilling a dark stream across the tablecloth.

"I didn't think so." Sid leaned back in his chair, looking as relaxed as Ben was tense. "You imagine you can be so moral, denying your very nature to protect her. How long do you think that will last? How long do you think she could bear your youth as she begins to age?" He turned to Rhonda, again whispering, "Eternity."

Rhonda wove her fingers through Sidell's and smiled at Deirdre. "Don't you get it? He talks of something lasting—something for eternity. It's just what I always wanted."

Sid looked at Benton. "You see? Rhonda wants me. Doesn't Deirdre want you?"

Deirdre blushed. "Ben and I are friends."

Sid's long eyeeteeth gleamed in the candlelight when he smiled at her. "Nothing more? I can offer you everything. Perhaps you would prefer me?"

"Certainly not!"

"Well, well, you two are quite a pair—strangling in your own morality." He held up a glass of wine and let the light gleam in the dark red liquid. "It looks like blood, doesn't it? It's what you want, isn't it Benton? Give in to your nature—you know you can't deny it forever." He took a slow swallow, licked his lips, and passed the glass to Benton.

Benton pushed the wine aside. "I think nature is something we can rise above if we are *men*. Animals, of course, can't. I do what I have to do. It doesn't really matter what I want." He stood up and took Deirdre's hand. "Come on, I think we better leave."

Deirdre looked at her friend. "Rhonda, do you want to come home with me tonight?"

Rhonda looked into Sid's eyes. "No thanks. I'm fine right here."

Ben and Deirdre walked home, each lost in separate thoughts and hardly aware of the penetrating cold until they arrived at their doorstep with Deirdre shivering.

"Come into my apartment," Ben invited, "I'll make us something hot to drink."

She sat on the couch while he boiled water and spooned herbs into a pot. "What would happen if you moved? If you were away from this Enclave, maybe you wouldn't have such a struggle with your feelings."

"I have moved—frequently—as a cover. I can't let any comments circulate about how I 'don't look a day over . . . whatever.' Sooner or later someone would get suspicious. I like to work; it's the only connection I have with life. So I move every few years, change jobs, change my name."

"What about your ID? Doesn't it have your date of birth?"

"It's not all that hard to get a fake Social Security Number if you know where to go. I don't drive or use credit cards, so I keep things pretty simple." He covered his face with his hands. "It all sounds so shoddy. Like I'm some kind of crook."

She smiled, trying to lighten the mood. "Or maybe a spy—always on the run—hiding out from the bad guys."

"That makes it sound glamorous—it isn't. And the bottom line is I'm still a vampire. And there will always be other vampires who will find me. Where ever I've gone, Sidell has arrived within two or three days." He grimaced. "They network very well."

She took the cup of tea and blew across the steaming surface. "How can I help? I talked to Father More after Mass one day. He says there must be a way—if you want it."

"It's such a conflict." He paced. "I have to feed. It isn't just lust—it's hunger as well. But I don't want to be a predator." He sat next to her, reaching for her hand, but then not taking it. "I've never been able to talk to anyone before. I don't get close to people as a rule. If I keep my distance, no one gets hurt."

"But surely, in all these years, in all the places you've been, you've had other friends."

"Yeah. Look what happened with Sidell. I'm cut off from friendships. It's another consequence." He picked up his cup, avoiding her eyes as he drank.

"Then what am I? Just a consequence?" She touched his shoulder, but he still wouldn't meet her eyes. "I thought we were friends—I want to be friends." Tears overflowed down her cheeks and she drew a shaky breath that turned into a sob.

He looked up at the sound, his eyes dark with sorrow. "You weep? Oh, Deirdre, don't cry for me. I don't deserve it—I'm a monster."

"But I know a Benton Colyer who's a man—and it is the man I weep for, not the monster. I pray for you—for that Benton—every day." She stood up. "Thank you for the tea. I think I better go home now."

"Good night." He reached out to her, but she turned away before he could touch her, and stumbled out the door.

EIGHT

Deirdre answered the knock at her door to find Benton holding a thick envelope. She hadn't seen him in a couple of days and she flung the door open.

"Benton! Hi, how are you? Come on in."

He paused at the threshold. "Are you sure?"

"Of course." She chewed her lip. "I have to apologize for that outburst the other night."

"Oh . . . me, too. I think I got carried away." He followed her into the room.

She grinned. "I guess that makes us even."

"Good. Because there's a favor I need to ask you." He handed her the envelope. "I know this is short notice, but I'd like you to be my guest."

She pulled the stiff, engraved note card out of the envelope. "This is an invitation for the Charity Gala."

"Yes. As a local celebrity, I'm expected to make an appearance. I thought you might like to come with me . . . if you could get the night off work . . . if you had a gown . . . well, that's a lot of ifs." He smiled.

"Oh, I'd love to go. I'll have to ask Shelley, but I think it will be okay. I mean this is big—they'll understand. And I can borrow a gown from stock—if you don't mind that I wear something old."

"Well, is it older than me?" His eyes twinkled.

She giggled. "No, it's from the 30's—a fabulous one all beaded on top with miles of chiffon in the skirt. Oh Ben!" She jumped up and hugged him.

"I have to admit it will be nice to have a date." He seemed a little overwhelmed by her enthusiasm.

"I'll go in early tonight and ask. I can let you know after work."

"Great. Thank you, Deirdre. I'm pleased you want to come."

"Thank you for asking me. This is so exciting!"

Deirdre flew into the shop an hour early brandishing the invitation. "I have a huge favor to ask. I need Saturday night off. I've been invited to the Charity Gala."

Mitch raised an eyebrow. "Would it be with Benton?"

"Yes," she answered. "What do you think?"

He shrugged. "You *have* to go."

"It's up to you guys—someone will need to run the show."

"I'll do it," Barb offered. "In fact I can stay tonight and learn the set up."

"Shelley? You're the boss."

"Looks to me like it's all settled." Shelley nodded. "Except for one very important thing. What are you planning to wear? Cinderella can't go in jeans."

"Well, I had been thinking of the chiffon gown with the beaded top."

"Go try it on. If it needs alterations, I'll fix it tonight."

"Thanks, Shelley. You're a doll." Deirdre ran to the wardrobe room to find the gown.

Mitch watched as they pinned and adjusted. "Do you have shoes?"

Deirdre nodded. "Gold sandals."

"Perfect. They'll complement the gold in the beading. Have you thought about your hair?"

"Oh, no—I'll never get an appointment this late." Deirdre shoved her fingers into the mass of tangled curls. "I guess I'll have to go as is."

Mitch shook his head. "Not if I can help it. You be here at noon Saturday and I'll do your hair and make-up." He picked up her hand and examined it. "Your nails too. When did you last have a manicure?"

"Actually, I've never had one."

Mitch's eyebrows shot up to his hairline. "No kidding—well, this is a good time to start. I think an iridescent gold polish will be nice—especially if you have gold sandals."

"You're not going to do my toes too?"

"Of course I am, my dear, it's the details that count. And that's what makes me so good at what I do."

Mitch was the hair, millinery and accessories coordinator and he wasn't bragging. His hats were period confections and actresses often found compacts and hankies in their purses, even if they weren't required props. He said it made them feel the part better if they didn't have to pretend about ordinary items. Details were Mitch's forte. Deirdre counted on him to have jewelry pulled from their stock for her as well.

Barb grabbed her arm. "I just heard them call half-hour. Leave all this to the experts—we have a show to run."

Benton agreed to pick Deirdre up at the theater at six o'clock so they could meet the radio station owner and his wife for dinner. Ben said it was a long-standing tradition for him to eat with his boss.

At noon, she packed a tote bag with her sandals, lingerie and hose, hoping she hadn't forgotten anything important. Mitch had all the makeup and hair accessories she would need.

She slipped on her favorite ring—the antique one her parents gave her for her sixteenth birthday. The onyx cameo surrounded by tiny diamonds would certainly meet with Mitch's approval. Dressed now in her jeans and sweater, she definitely felt like Cinderella. And Shelley, Barb and Mitch were her fairy godparents.

Mitch wrapped her in a dressing gown—"Just like a spa, dear"—and got right down to the job. He gave her a facial and trimmed her split ends. Deirdre enjoyed the fun of having someone work on her all afternoon, but her stomach fluttered with anticipation all the same. The Charity Gala filled more than the society page; it was a headline news item.

She looked at the finished product in the mirror. Mitch had pulled her hair up, but let it tumble in a rippling cascade with tiny curls framing her face. Rhinestones sparkled at ears, neck and wrists and her finger and toenails gleamed. Mitch handed her an evening bag with hanky and a red rose for Ben's boutonniere.

She gasped her thanks. "I've been so nervous, I never thought of a flower for him."

"My pleasure," he answered. "That's why I'm the detail man."

Barb showed up before six, in time to see how Deirdre looked before setting up for the show. She brought Benton up to the costume shop with her.

"Prince Charming is here, Cinderella," she called as they came through the door.

Deirdre felt her face grow warm as she turned to greet him.

"Wow," they said together. Ben, as usual, wore impeccable black and white. She thought what a shabby backdrop the cluttered shop was for his formal splendor.

"You look lovely," he added as she twirled letting the yards of chiffon swirl around her ankles.

"I don't think you've seen me in a dress before."

"You wore one the day you wanted me to come to Mass with you."

"Oh, yes, I remember." She smiled at him. "You noticed."

"I notice lots of things." He touched one of the curls on her forehead. "I notice how your hair is made for candlelight. It makes it look like molten gold."

"Thank you, Ben."

"You're welcome. I hope you like red—I thought any color flower would go with a gown of gold and ivory." He slid a corsage of dark red roses and baby's breath on her wrist.

"It's perfect, thank you." She fastened Ben's rose on his lapel.

"It's cold out. You'll need this." Mitch draped a cape around her bare shoulders.

Deirdre stroked the fur collar. "This is the cloak from *Little Foxes.*"

"Yes, and since all it did was hang on the set for an act, I think it needs to see the light of day—or in this case night. Go show it off!"

"Thank you all for everything." Deirdre hugged her friends and took Benton's arm as he led her to a waiting taxi.

The driver headed for the main entrance, but Benton asked him to pull up at an unobtrusive door on a side street. "I hope you aren't offended—the press isn't allowed in the hotel, so they swamp the main entrance. I prefer to sneak in this way."

He held the door for her and helped her out of the car. Deirdre felt a twinge of regret that she wouldn't have a photograph of this memorable evening.

As they mounted the steps to the hotel, Benton spotted a single newsman lurking by the door. He put his hand over the camera lens. "You know the deal, Jerry. No pictures and I'll give you an interview."

"Benton, have a heart. This is the first year you've brought a date. I gotta have a shot." Jerry tried to wrest the camera from Benton's hand without damaging the lens.

"No, you don't." Benton stared him down.

"Just the lady then?" Jerry looked over Benton's shoulder to catch Deirdre's eye.

"That's up to her." Benton opened the door and ducked inside.

Deirdre posed, hugging the fur close to her chin and smiling. The camera clicked twice and she followed Ben into the hotel.

They checked their wraps and made their way across the foyer to the banquet hall. Deirdre clung to his arm as he greeted business acquaintances and introduced her. His easy acceptance of the formal atmosphere drew her smoothly into the scene. They sat for dinner with the owner who entertained them with stories from his years in the radio business. Deirdre had a few stories of her own about famous and not-so-famous actors and their foibles that she added to the meld.

Deirdre tightened her grip on Benton's arm as they entered the ballroom. She needed to feel his steady presence as she gazed around.

"It's all right to blink," Benton whispered.

"I've never seen anything so beautiful." She smiled at him, and then looked around again. The wood paneled walls gleamed and the ceiling was jeweled with crystal chandeliers. Each corner seemed to be heaped with pink and white flowers which scented the air as they passed. Along the walls were tables for each charity displaying its function and the items for the auction that would take place later. Everything sparkled.

At the far end was a buffet table heaped with sweet and savory desserts. Benton served her a cup of coffee, and she savored the hot drink. "Would you like dessert now?" he asked.

"Maybe later." She finished the coffee and set down the cup. "Right now I'd like to dance."

"I'll have to dance with other ladies," Ben mentioned as he led her to the dance floor. "But I will dance the first dance with you, and, I promise, the last. Then as many as I can fit in between. But I don't think you'll have to sit out much."

"Ben, that reporter said this was the first time you've brought a date. Why doesn't an eligible bachelor like you know any other women?"

"I never bothered to cultivate relationships. And any women I've met on my own were merely . . . um," he paused.

"One bite stands?"

"Touché. And to be honest, I usually chose . . ."

"It's okay, Benton. I can imagine."

"Maybe you shouldn't. I don't want you to think badly of me. It was strictly a hunter/prey situation — nothing intimate." He groaned softly. "That didn't sound much better."

"I understand." She shook her head. "It is an odd thing to come to terms with the fact that my boyfriend is a . . . *vampire.*" She whispered the last word.

"Your boyfriend? Really?" He smiled his closed-lip smile as he took her hand and led her to the dance floor. "And you are the first woman I've ever wanted to share my life."

The music began and he swept her into the rhythm of the dance. She had never had such an accomplished partner. No clinched swaying from side to side like some of the couples, he knew the waltz, and he knew how to lead her around the floor. She relaxed into his firm grip and followed.

"Where did you learn to dance like this?" She fanned herself breathlessly as the dance ended.

"Why, Miss Deirdre, *when* Ah come from," he winked and broadened his southern accent, "all well-bred young men learn how to dance. And since well-bred hostesses insist on having more men than women at their balls, we all have plenty of opportunities to display our skills."

"How strange that you remember those long-ago days. The world has changed a lot since then."

"It has—some for the better, some for the worse." He guided her into the next dance.

"Wasn't there a girl back then—one you were fond of?"

"Well, there were two. I liked them, and they seemed to have their sights set on me. But knowing I would be called to war, I didn't want to make a commitment. I certainly didn't want to leave a widow."

"What happened to them? Do you know?"

"They married, grew old, died, like everyone else." He shrugged, but his face seemed to close over the pain.

"I'm sorry."

"But here I am—with you. How can I have regrets? Maybe after all these years, this is where the roads led." His fingers curled gently around hers as they dipped and turned under the glittering chandeliers.

"Do you really think so?" She followed, lost in the romance of the music.

"I might be merely enchanted by the magic of this night—but yes, I do think so. There is something special about you, Deirdre."

"Oh, thank you, Ben."

"And now, I hate to say it, but duty calls. I'll be back when I can." With his hand on his chest, he bowed.

"I'll look forward to it."

The station owner stepped up, with two glasses of champagne and asked for the next dance. "I may not be as graceful as Benton," he warned. "He's not only a good dancer; he has a charm that makes him adept at this kind of public relations. But don't be fooled, he'd rather be with you"

Deirdre finished her wine, and let the dance carry them around the floor. She had another dance or two with Benton, and they sampled the desserts. Deirdre liked the tarts with raspberry filling, but Benton preferred the cheese cannoli.

After another dance, Benton left her to make the rounds and Deirdre found herself with the director from the theater.

"My dear, what a pleasant surprise."

"It's nice to see you, too, Ambrose."

He led her into a faultlessly correct mamba. "I have a burning question. If you're here, who's running the show?"

"Barbara offered to do it for me." Deirdre skillfully managed to avoid stepping on her boss's toes.

"Did she? Excellent. But tell me how our humble wardrobe mistress got invited to the Charity Gala." He seemed to eye the other couples as they danced.

"I'm a guest of Benton Colyer."

Ambrose raised an eyebrow. "My, my, Deirdre, that's quite a conquest. I thought he didn't like girls."

"He likes girls." Deirdre took a steadying breath, "He happens to be a very private person."

"All right, all right, you don't have to bristle." Ambrose's technical skill on the dance floor felt lacking in warmth or flair. "He's an enigma. But then, I've known him for years—he likes to keep us guessing."

Benton tapped Ambrose on the shoulder. "May I cut in?"

Deirdre pulled away from her partner. "Ambrose, I believe you know Benton Colyer. Benton, Ambrose is the artistic director at the theater."

"It's a pleasure to meet the man behind the curtain." Benton extended his hand.

"The pleasure is all mine," Ambrose replied. "Now I'll leave you two to your dance."

Benton took Deirdre in his arms. "I promised you the last dance, and here I am. Thank you for being so patient with me."

"Oh, Ben, thank *you*! This has been the most wonderful night of my life. I wish it didn't have to end." She hated the idea of putting on her wrap and going home.

"It doesn't have to end yet—we could sneak out before the auction and go to Luigi's for a late supper."

She smiled. "And stop at the bookstore to show Marvin how elegant we look?"

"Of course."

"Then let's go." He held out her wrap.

NINE

The night at the Gala had been like a dream, but the moon set to make way for the dawn and Deirdre needed to abandon her pumpkin coach and face the day. She had important work to do. Sidell wasn't like Benton, cursing his vampire existence; Sidell relished every chance he got to prey and increase the undead numbers. She had to warn her friend, but it wasn't going to be easy. As she headed to work her hands grew cold with trepidation as well as the weather.

Deirdre saw Rhonda's coat in the office and managed to track her down in the ladies room. "You have to get away from Sidell."

"Right." Rhonda shook her head. "Will you make up your mind? I meet a man who's serious for once and now you tell me to leave him? No way." She blasted hot water into the sink and scrubbed her hands. "He said he was going to pick out a ring. In case you hadn't noticed, that means marriage. And let me tell you, I have no trouble spending eternity with a guy who looks like Sidell does."

"Eternity." Deirdre put a hand on her friend's arm. "I'm just not sure he means what you think he means."

"Eternity—as in forever—as in 'till death do us part." Rhonda counted each item off on her fingers. "What about that don't you understand?"

"Maybe death won't part you . . ." Deirdre groaned, as Rhonda looked blank. "I'm not doing very well am I?"

"No, honey, you're not." She rummaged in her bag. "Where is my blush? I can't believe how pale I am." She flicked the brush over her cheeks. "Much better. What makes you such an authority on Sidell anyway?"

"Benton told me about him. They've known each other for a long time. Can't you see what he's doing to you? Don't you know why you're so pale?" Deirdre turned Rhonda to face the mirror and pushed aside her collar. Two tiny red marks showed on her neck.

"So what? That is just a love bite. Unlike you and Benton, Sid and I have an intimate relationship, if you know what that means." She flipped her collar back over the wounds and began sweep a brush though her hair. "Besides, it doesn't hurt—what's the big deal?"

"It's not just a love bite. Sidell is a vampire."

"Give me a break, girl. How many horror movies have you been watching?" She spritzed a little body spray behind her ears. "Vampires. Ha! You don't believe that stuff, do you?"

"Actually, I do. Rhonda, you're my friend, I care about you." Deirdre pulled paper towels from the dispenser as she watched her friend in the mirror.

"I know you do, girl, but Sid said Benton might get you to spin some way-out tale." She rolled her eyes.

"I know it sounds way-out," Deirdre said. "And that's not the half of it. He wants to make you into a vampire—just like he is."

"I'm not listening," Rhonda sang out as she crammed her stuff back in her purse.

"So there's no point in my telling you to drive a stake through his heart?"

"No! Jeez, you're certifiable. First of all, I happen to be in love with him. Secondly, I don't suppose you've heard that *murder* is *illegal* in this state?"

"Of course I've heard that. But it isn't murder if he's already dead." Deirdre pointed out.

"Deirdre, go home. Dead people don't walk and talk and make love to their girlfriends. Get a grip on reality. Take a pill or a drink, whatever you like, just get over it!"

"Okay. I tried. No hard feelings?"

"I guess not." Rhonda stormed out of the room, banging the door as she went.

Deirdre splashed her face with a handful of cold water. *This* is *reality, girl.* Rhonda was the one who didn't believe. Who could she talk to? Maybe Father More would believe her.

* * * *

Deirdre let the last notes of the postlude wash over her as the service ended and the organist finished playing. The beads of her rosary slid through her fingers, clinking softly, but she was counting thoughts instead of prayers. She sighed and tried to start over. Father More slid into the pew next to her.

"Is there anything I can do for you, Deirdre?" He asked.

"Probably not, Father. I think . . . no, I *am* in love."

"Most young girls find that a time for rejoicing—unless, of course, the young man does not return the sentiment."

"But he does return the feelings."

"Still, there *is* a problem?" Father More had a soothing voice.

Deirdre sniffed and hunted in her pocket for a tissue. "Well . . . he's a vampire."

"Hmm." He tapped a finger on his lips. Whatever he thought of that statement, Deirdre couldn't tell. "I take it you are not speaking metaphorically?"

"No, I'm not." She drew the crystal beads back and forth through her fingers, not meeting his eyes. "You seem to understand the paranormal." She looked up. "I thought you would believe me."

"I do, Deirdre." Father More nodded. "Now your questions the other day make sense."

She sighed with relief and blew her nose in the soggy tissue. "Yes. Oh, Father, is there anything I can do?"

"Let's go to my study where we can talk privately." He led the way to the rectory next door. "Can I fix you a cup of tea?"

"Thank you, I'd like that." She wandered around the comfortable room looking at the neatly shelved horror books. Somehow she found his knowledge of the weird and wonderful to be comforting.

He handed her a steaming mug. "So, you're in love with a vampire."

"Yes, the more I realize that, the more confused I get. I didn't know Benton was a vampire at first—well, there were signs, I know that now, but I didn't want to consider them. He was polite, interesting, and fun to be with."

"Handsome?"

"Father!" she exclaimed.

"Well?" He raised an eyebrow.

"All right, yes, he is handsome." She grinned. "Then I caught him feeding one night and the whole story came out. The thing is: he doesn't want to be a vampire."

"A stake in the heart would easily release him from that existence." Father More took a seat across from her.

She gaped in horror. "And release him from everything else in the process. I don't think that's what he wants—I know it's not what I want."

He sipped his tea. "Benton wants to live, but without the vampire curse—that's understandable. What do you want?"

"I want things to be normal—to live with him, be his wife, have his children."

"If the curse is broken, I don't know what will happen to his body. Do you know how old he is?"

She shrugged. "He told me he has lived as a vampire over one hundred and forty years. He seems to be in his twenties."

"Oh dear," he muttered, "in the normal scheme of things, he'd be long deceased by now."

"So if he is restored, would he turn back into . . . a mutilated corpse?" She shuddered.

"I don't know. A vampire that is destroyed disintegrates. But if he is restored, he might be allowed to finish out the life he has right now. I don't know of any precedent to study." Father More finished his tea and set down the cup. "One thing he must do is give up his vampire desires. Do you know if he is able to do that?"

"He has for short times. Then he said he feels so empty, sooner or later he must have blood."

"Blood. I see. Doesn't he realize that only the Blood of our Lord will satisfy him?"

"The Blood of Jesus. Of course." Deirdre allowed herself to smile. "But he says he is cursed. God has no place for him now."

"God has a place for him, but he must renounce the curse and try to overcome the cravings."

She sighed. "I thought maybe my love could satisfy those cravings."

"Your love can't do that, but it may be what he needs to turn back to God. Be careful—if you stay with him, you also must resist the temptation to follow his path."

"I may love a vampire, Father, but I don't want to be one."

"The longer you're with him, the harder it will become to avoid. He will begin to put pressure on you. You said he is handsome; already he has wielded his physical attraction. You have your own desires. Can you give them up to lead him to the truth? It won't be easy.

"You spoke of a home and family—that would imply a certain level of intimacy." He tapped his clerical collar. "This doesn't make me immune to the desires of the flesh, not does it protect me from the machinations of the world. I can imagine how you are feeling. How long can you stay chaste?"

"Chaste? Do you mean celibate?" She stared at her entwined fingers. "But I thought maybe if I married him . . ."

He shook his head. "Marriage involves a physical union—two people untied in spirit and flesh. Ultimately, to unite with a vampire is to become one yourself."

Father More passed her a box of tissues and put a gentle hand on her shoulder.

"I wanted a happy ending," she sobbed.

"But the real happy ending comes when we meet our Savior beyond the river. And that is so much more than the few decades we inhabit this earth. What our bodies have here and now is nothing compared with what our soul gets in heaven. And we're talking about Benton's soul, my dear."

"You're right." She sniffed bravely and wiped her eyes. "What do you want me to do?"

"Bring him to me."

TEN

Benton paced. *Dead of night, dead of night.* The church clock rang out two chimes. *Dead of night, dead of night.*

He gave a bitter laugh. "I am the Dead of Night. I haven't tasted blood for weeks. Why can't I resist the burning hunger that consumes me?"

He stepped out of his apartment and stopped in front of Deirdre's door. Since she had invited him in, her home was open to him. He turned his head; the hall was deserted. But he had hardly expected anyone to wander the corridor at this time.

With a sigh, he let out his breath and slipped between the door and the frame into her room. He shook himself as he re-materialized, and blinked, accustoming his eyes to the shadowy room. She lay sleeping, her bed in a pool of moonlight the only bright spot in the gloom.

He sat down beside her and smoothed her tousled hair. His hand looked skeletal in the pale light—the fire of his unsatisfied cravings had pared flesh from his already spare frame and he felt like he was made of parchment stretched over bone. But there would always be something left—he could never die.

Deirdre looked beautiful in slumber and she smiled as he touched her. She stirred something inside him—perhaps reminding him of something he missed. It had been so long since he had befriended another person. The vampire pact bound him inextricably to Sidell, but Benton did not care to be his companion and never sought out that type of connection with other vampires. In 140 years, he had forgotten how it felt to be loved.

She smelled like spring rain and he bent closer, letting his lips brush her neck, his teeth pierce her throat. A drop of blood lay on his tongue. He gasped at the sweet, metallic taste, and leaped up from the bed.

How could he do that? She wanted him to change, and he wanted to do it. He tried to turn aside from his nature, but in the end, he betrayed her. She let him in—wept for him—and in return he feeds? She prayed for him, how could he prey on her? He couldn't stay in her room another moment.

He slid through the crack beneath the window and stood on the fire escape. From six stories up he could see across the city and cold night air fanned his face. His body throbbed, a cadence of unfulfilled longings, and he knew he would not rest that night until he fed. He spread his arms and jumped, his coat swirling around him like prehistoric wings.

He knew where to go, where bars and strip joints lined the streets and the lost and broken sold their bodies behind the cheap hotels. He found a victim easily.

"Don't you want to go inside? Maybe have a drink?" She cast a hopeful glance at the doorway of a nearby bar.

"You can have a drink later. We won't be long," he answered beckoning her down a deserted alley.

"Whatever—it's your dime." She followed him to a sheltered doorway.

He smiled a little, not showing his teeth, and gazed into her eyes. She nodded, mesmerized, and leaned against him. He could use her now and she would never remember. He sank his teeth into her neck and drank.

Deirdre's blood had been pure, this woman's had a taint of alcohol, but he didn't care. He felt delight and cool strength as he drew nourishment from her, and when she grew weak, he eased her onto an abandoned carton.

"Is everything okay?" a voice called from the corner. In that part of town, the streetwalkers commonly watched out for each other.

"It's fine," he answered, "but I could use your help. She seems a little faint."

The girl quickly picked her way down the alley.

Benton smiled at her, licking his lips. "Everything will be all right."

"Of course." She closed her eyes.

How long had it been since he fed twice in one evening? He couldn't recall.

"Why did I fast so long?" He knew only strength flowing through his veins, a pulse of vitality he had long forgotten and now embraced. He turned away from the alley, back to the street and encountered a familiar figure.

"So. The preacher falls."

"Sidell." Benton wasn't surprised; it was just his luck to pick the most populated alley in town. His coat swung around his ankles as he strode. "What concern is it of yours?"

Sidell waited where the glow from the streetlamp highlighted his golden hair. "Oh, no concern, just interesting. You say one thing, and practice another. It seems nature wins out after all."

"I was starving." Benton glanced behind.

"Oh, I know." Sid showed his teeth. "You don't have to justify yourself with me—in fact you could join me. Or have you had enough?" He eyed the two women huddled on the box.

It was not enough. "Let's go." He had tasted blood—fed well, in fact—but he was not yet satiated. Tonight Benton Colyer would gorge. Sidell led the way.

* * * *

"What have you been doing lately?" Deirdre hadn't seen Ben for a few days, but tonight she curled contentedly on his couch, a steaming mug of tea in her hand.

"Oh, not much—the usual—you know." Ben left a scented candle burning while he puttered in the kitchen fixing food, then set a tray on a low table next to her. She thought he looked better than he had recently—not so gaunt and consumed—and he radiated energy.

She blew on her tea and sipped. "I had the strangest dream the other night."

"What was it about?" He picked up his mug.

"You."

"Really?" When he grinned, his eyeteeth—longer and sharper than she recalled—glinted in the candlelight.

"Yes. I drifted beyond the sea of dreams, feeling the prick of falling stars against my skin as if I were larger than the heavens. Then you flew out of the blackness of the night and touched me. The stars became stars again; the planets whirled in their dance around me as I swam back to earth.

"Suddenly I dwindled back into my own size, back onto my own bed and looking up, I saw myself reflected in your eyes. You leaned closer and closer—I held out my arms, and I thought you were going to kiss me. Then I opened my eyes, and you were gone. But the ache that remained was beautiful. I lay staring at the ceiling while tears filled my eyes and ran down my cheeks into my ears." Deirdre looked down as her face grew warm.

He drank some tea. "It sounds . . . as if you wanted me to kiss you."

"I did." She moved closer to him. "I do."

He set down his cup and she slid her arms around him. He closed his eyes, and frowned a little, as if trying to remember what a kiss was.

"It's like this," she whispered and pressed her lips to his. It seemed to come naturally to both of them — tender lips, soft breath, and a feeling deep within that spoke of something sacred.

She pulled back and looked into his eyes. "I like that."

"I do too." He held her close to his body, leaning into another kiss, opening his heart. "What is this, Deirdre? I've never felt like this before."

"I love you, Benton. Don't you understand?"

"And that's what this warm stirring is — love?"

"Of course it is." She tangled her fingers in his hair.

"I've missed something." His fingers trembled as they slid down her neck and across her shoulder. "I didn't know this is what I wanted."

She laid her head on his chest and wrapped her arms around him, tended and contented. "I'm glad you realize it now."

"But it's too late. I can't have it — I can't have you!" His voice sounded raw, hoarse with unshed tears.

"But you *can* have me. I'm here, and I want you."

Gently, he pushed her aside. "I have to tell you what I did the other night — to confess. I came in your room. Oh, you may have shot the bolt, but when you invited me in, you left the door open to me—one of attributes of a vampire is to pass through a crack. You did see me, but I didn't come to kiss you. I came to feed. I bit you."

Deirdre's hand stroked her neck where a tiny mark showed pink on her skin. "I thought this was an insect bite."

"No, it was me. But I promise you I didn't feed—not on you. One drop is all I tasted." He wiped his face. "I hope you can believe that.

"I didn't want to betray you further so I left. Then the blood lust overcame me. That night I fed . . ." he shook his head, "no . . . I gorged. The two victims I found should have been enough, but then I encountered Sidell."

He covered his face, struggling to continue. "He took me with him. I couldn't resist any more. I felt so powerful as I drank, savoring every drop. You have to understand that while I feed, I enjoy it. And finally the cravings stopped." He held his hands out to her, slender, but no longer skeletal. "You can see how I am now—filled and alive. I don't think I can exist as a husk anymore."

"If you give up blood," she shuddered as she said it, "you need to be filled with something else. Can't it be my love? Isn't it strong enough for both of us?"

"It might be for a while, until the unavoidable pain of the vampire nature reasserts itself. Sooner or later, I will break faith with you. Sooner or later, I will feed on you. Please, Deirdre, leave me now. We have to say goodnight."

"All right, if you insist, I'll go. But I mean it, Ben—I love you. I'm right across the hall."

He sighed. "I know."

ELEVEN

Deirdre gathered the last of the laundry and lugged the basket upstairs to the costume shop. As she sorted clothes into the washer, something in the hamper that didn't seem to belong caught her eye. She bent over, searching through the socks and tee shirts until she found a dainty handkerchief.

It wasn't one of Mitch's props—it was one of a set she had given Rhonda for Christmas. She remembered finding them at the vintage clothing boutique. Unusual—real linen with Art Deco appliques—they had been yellow with age, but whitened beautifully when she washed them.

Deirdre fingered the soft fabric and wondered how it ended up in the laundry. Rhonda had brought her a croissant and a cappuccino that night. Maybe it fell when she left the food on the prop table. Deirdre shrugged and dropped the handkerchief into the sudsy water. She'd iron it and return it to Rhonda tomorrow—they had plans to meet for lunch. No doubt, the mystery would be solved.

* * * *

The waitress brought their entrees—the pasta special for the day. Rhonda ordered a glass of wine and offered to treat Deirdre, but she refused. The eggplant Parmesan alone suited her fine.

"Look what I found." Deirdre held out the trophy. "You must have dropped it backstage yesterday."

"I didn't." Rhonda took the hanky and examined it carefully. "I remember taking this *out* of my purse and leaving it on the dresser before I went to work."

"Maybe one of the actresses has one just like it. I'll take it back."

"No, this is mine. I can tell by this little hole." She smoothed the hanky flat on the table. "And there's the spot of blood I couldn't quite wash out. This is definitely mine. I wonder how it got there?"

Deirdre had an idea lurking at the back of her mind. "Was Sid with you yesterday?"

"He was. That's what I've been dying to tell you." Rhonda beamed. "We're engaged." She displayed her left hand with an impressive diamond gleaming on her third finger.

"It's gorgeous." Deirdre wondered how the undead could buy a ring like that. Then she remembered a news flash about a recent burglary at a downtown jewelry store.

104

"It is, isn't it? Sid has fabulous taste." Rhonda turned her hand so the stone would flash in the light. "We haven't set a date, but I'm thinking of June or July for the wedding, after the season here closes, so I have time to plan and we can take a proper honeymoon."

Deirdre felt weak. "Congratulations." How far had things gone between them?

"And that's not all." Rhonda leaned across the table, whispering. "This is totally secret, okay?"

Deirdre nodded.

"I think I'm pregnant. I don't want to tell Sid until I know for certain, so don't say a word. Isn't that wonderful news?"

"Wonderful." Deirdre thought of words to describe how she felt—cold and frightened came to mind—but they didn't seem appropriate to the occasion.

"He's planning to move in with me next week. I know you don't approve of us living together, but he's the *only* guy for me." Rhonda babbled on, "I'm unbelievably in love. Everything is perfect between Sid and me, now with a baby coming, the three of us will be together. I've never been happier—you have to be happy, too, okay, Deirdre?

Happy? "Oh, Rhonda, you know I want the best for you." How can Rhonda have a baby with Sidell? She tried to focus on Father More's words about the dangers of a physical union with a vampire. She would do anything . . . almost anything . . . to have a baby with Benton.

"I'm going to look at bridal gowns this weekend. I want a style that will look nice if I'm showing by the wedding." Rhonda leaned back in her chair and caressed her flat stomach, a dreamy, half-asleep look in her eyes. "In fact, I hope the baby does show. Wouldn't that be cute?"

Cute? Deirdre blurted, "Rhonda, this doesn't sound like you. If things are so perfect, why wait? You could get married now and still have a honeymoon in June. I realize you must be thrilled with everything that's been going on, but how can you be so blasé about an unplanned pregnancy?"

"Well, it isn't *exactly* unplanned—I just never took precautions." She still had a dreamy smile. "I want Sid's baby. Who cares if we're not married?"

"Rhonda!"

She jumped. "Deirdre, you don't understand. It's Sid. He's . . . irresistible. When we're together, all I can think about is what I can do for him, how to please him."

"And that means sex?" Deirdre tried to wipe the frown off her face.

"Oh . . . well, yes . . . that's part of it, of course. But, he's wonderful, and he treats me well. How can I complain? Look." Ronda pulled back her hair to reveal the jewels sparkling at her ears. She wore a diamond pendant as well, and Deirdre noticed the freshly reddened wounds on her throat as she opened her blouse.

Doesn't she see what he's doing to her?

"Being engaged is great—" Rhonda twisted her ring, centering it precisely on her finger, "—But being engaged *and* pregnant is the icing on the wedding cake."

"How are your parents taking this?"

"They're delighted—they adore Sid. And once they find out about the baby, they'll adjust to the idea."

"I thought you weren't sure of the pregnancy. Now you sound pretty positive."

"Well, I haven't done a test yet, but my period's *never* late. I'm tired all the time and sometimes queasy in the morning. What else could it be?"

A little too much nightlife with a vampire? Clearly Sidell was using her. "I don't know . . . but I won't spread the word until you say it's okay." Deirdre winced at the almost-lie. *I'll have to tell Ben.*

"I know you don't like Sid, but put that aside and be my maid-of-honor, please?"

"Of course I will, if that's what you want." Deirdre agreed.

"Thanks, honey." Rhonda tucked the hanky in her purse and stood up. "You and Ben might think along the same lines—I highly recommend it!"

But what is she recommending—engagement or pregnancy?

* * * *

Deirdre tried to call Benton, but he didn't answer. He only turned off his cell phone at work or while he was sleeping. On a Saturday afternoon, she suspected the latter. His voice mail kicked in.

"Ben, it's Deirdre. We have to talk. I'll see you at home after work. Be there, please?" As she hung up, she wondered if the last sentence sounded a little desperate.

She strolled through the discount store at the mall to do some needed shopping—perusing the selection of scented shampoos and textured pantyhose seemed easier than pondering Rhonda's fate.

As she passed the maternity store, she stopped and looked in the window. "Why am I not surprised to see a bridal gown?" she muttered.

The mannequin even had a padded belly to display the full effect of the dress. It was pretty, but not cute. Maybe Deirdre was trapped in the net of her traditional upbringing, but she didn't think a bride should be pregnant. Although she longed for intimacy with Benton, her heart and her head knew she should wait.

She took her purchases to the theater.

The show ran smoothly that night, with only the usual crises—lost buttons, broken shoelaces and laddered hose. Deirdre kept a back-up supply of all those little items.

As she hung up the costumes from the last quick-change, she noticed something on her wardrobe table. A single flower lay draped across her pre-set notebook, the petals—red so dark they were almost black—curled into a tight bud, and a white bow tied around the stem.

It wasn't a ribbon. It was a handkerchief—the mate of the one she had given Rhonda. The mate of the one she found yesterday. She gasped, a barely concealed shriek, tore off her apron and threw it over the rose. Who could have left it? The actors were all still on stage.

Sid! He must have come in during the third act. No one but cast and crew were allowed backstage during the performance. Could he have gained entrance through the Enclave? The actors hadn't mentioned seeing a stranger.

She picked up the apron with the same care she'd use to uncover a deadly insect. Sidell could not have sent a clearer message: He was near . . . He was watching . . . He had Rhonda.

"What a lovely rose. Those black ones smell delicious when they open." One of the actresses noticed her gift. "You must have a secret admirer, how exciting. I'll get a vase—I have an extra one you can borrow."

By now most of the women in the cast were exclaiming over the unusual flower, so Deirdre let them trim it and put it in water. She left the vase in the green room. At least they could enjoy it. She stuffed the hankie in her pocket.

TWELVE

Deirdre pounded on Ben's door.

"I'm coming, you don't have to damage the woodwork." He opened the door. "I got your message, what's up?"

Never had anyone looked as safe and normal as Ben did at that moment. She stepped inside, closed the door and put her arms around him. "Oh, Ben, I'm so frightened. Just hold me."

"Okay, okay." He stroked her hair. "Tell me what happened."

"It's Sid . . . and Rhonda . . . I'm confused, Ben. Promise you'll keep me safe, okay?"

His hand trembled. "I can't make a promise like that, Deirdre. I wish I could. But right now I'll do all I can to help you. Start by telling me the story."

"I think Sid has been stalking me. I never see him, but I've found things—Rhonda's things—in places they shouldn't be. He can get in the theater, can't he?"

"I'm afraid he can. He's trying to scare you."

"He's succeeding." She let out a shuddering sigh.

"Come sit down." Ben loosened her grip on his waist and led her to the sofa. "What about Rhonda?"

"She and Sid are engaged. He gave her a beautiful ring—other jewelry as well. He's planning to move into her apartment next week." She tried to think of words that wouldn't break Rhonda's confidence. "Ben, could Rhonda be pregnant?"

"It's unlikely—at least not by Sidell. Vampires don't—um—breed like mortals. Our need for intimacy becomes blood-lust, and our gratification comes from feeding."

"I see. But she complained about being tired and sick in the morning."

Benton creased his forehead in thought. "Loss of blood and anemia would probably inhibit Rhonda's natural cycle, as well as make her feel ill. She might suspect a pregnancy."

"Why can't she see what he's doing to her? She doesn't even notice that she has raw, open wounds on her neck." Deirdre shivered.

"She probably thinks they're blemishes or insect bites—you did."

She touched her neck. "That was different. My wound was so small."

"Deirdre, do you know what I mean by *glamour*, in the old sense of the word?"

"Like—*gramarye*? A magic spell?"

"Exactly." Ben went on. "Vampires have a glamour that is very seductive. It's protection, and an enticement. It keeps people from discovering who we are while it draws them into our thrall. I know you feel some of that power in me, but trust me, I will never wield it over you. The fact that you know I'm a vampire keeps you on your guard. But all Rhonda sees is a boyfriend—handsome, generous, and sexy. That's all Sidell wants her to see. And Sidell has always been adept at using his looks and sexuality to serve his own ends. I know that very well."

Deirdre sighed. "You said he was a prostitute."

"Yes. He still is, but it's blood, not money or drugs he's after now."

"Is he going to make Rhonda into a vampire?"

"I believe so—he's marking her as his own, just the way I marked him."

"Is there anything we can do? She won't listen to me. Maybe her parents could take her home for a while—for her health?"

"Medical intervention would help—she'd certainly feel better, but the bond already started between her and Sid would draw her back to him. She'd seek him out, at any cost, and the cycle would begin again."

"But, Ben, we have to do something."

"If Sidell is destroyed before he makes her, she'll be restored to her former self."

"Destroyed? You mean . . ." Deirdre gestured as if driving a stake. "You aren't asking me to do that, are you?"

"It may come to that. If she's already a vampire, then she'll die as well. All those a vampire makes expire with him."

Deirdre didn't care for the implications. "If *you* were destroyed, then Sidell would die?"

Ben nodded.

"But what if you were *restored?* What would happen to them then?" she asked.

"Restored? To humanity?"

Deirdre nodded. "Isn't that what you want?" She took his hand and wrapped her warm fingers around his cool ones.

Ben looked at the knot of their intertwined fingers. "That might not be possible. I don't know of any precedent."

"Will you talk to Father More?"

"What can a priest do? He isn't going to listen to some crazy-sounding vampire story. Wouldn't that go against his beliefs?"

"Father More is different. He believes in listening—he believes in fighting evil. He wants to help us."

"Us?" Ben's eyes widened.

"Yes, I've told him about you—I guess I had to confess. He wants to meet you."

"I can't enter the sanctuary."

"Then meet us outside after mass tonight."

* * * *

Deirdre stopped Father More as they left the sanctuary. "Ben said he'd meet us—now—outside." She wiped tears that flooded her eyes with trembling fingers. "All of a sudden I feel so nervous. What are you going to say?"

Father More rested a gentle hand on her shoulder. "He's a lost sheep. I know what to say to them. And if he is here, then he probably wants to listen. It's in the Lord's hands."

She took a deep breath and followed him out the door.

THIRTEEN

Ben raised his hand in a wave as he saw Deirdre outside the church. He knew she would spot him. Even though the weather had begun to warm toward spring, he still wore his long coat and wide-brimmed hat. She ran down the steps to meet him and introduce the two men.

"Benton Colyer." Father More took his hand. "What a pleasure. I enjoy your radio show very much—it's nice to meet you in person. I'm Tom More."

"Deirdre's spoken of you often. I'm pleased to meet you, too, Father."

"I think I'll go," she said. "You two have a lot to talk about."

"Thanks for introducing us, Dee. I'll see you later." Ben squeezed her hand.

Father More put his hand on Benton's shoulder. "Deirdre said you can't enter the church building. Do you know why?"

"I believe there is a Guardian — a spirit that protects sacred places."

"Hmm. Interesting, I'll have to look that up." Father More seemed lost in thought for a moment. "There's a nice café around the corner, shall we go there and talk?"

"That sounds all right to me."

Father More led him to a booth at the back of the restaurant. "I don't know about you, but I'm hungry. Let's get some dinner — my treat."

After the waitress left with their orders, Father More turned business-like. "Deirdre tells me you were brought up in the church."

"I was, but that was before . . ." Ben stopped.

"Before you became a vampire." Father More finished.

"It sounds so odd to hear you say it like that, Father. You do understand this is not a game of make-believe, don't you?"

"Of course."

Benton rubbed his forehead. "Most people dismiss vampires as fiction."

Father More nodded. "But I have found much that we call fiction has a base in fact. So I try to keep my mind open enough to accept vampires as reality. Deirdre has told me a lot of your story."

"So, what do we do now?"

"When was the last time you made confession?"

"Before I enlisted in the Confederate Army. There isn't much time to attend Mass in the middle of a war.

And then, of course, I was shut out." Ben pleated his napkin.

"But now you want to return to the fold?"

"I wish I could."

"Our Father wants all his prodigals home." Father More sounded certain.

"But I turned my back, Father. It's been more than one hundred and forty years—a lot of time to sin," Benton said.

"Heavy burdens, my son."

"Including murder." Benton jabbed a fork into his food.

"Surely you don't mean the war. Are you speaking of Sidell? But he was . . ."

Ben shook his head. "Nothing you can say will justify making another person into a vampire. Maybe he wanted it—but I showed him the way."

"And that cuts you off from grace?"

"Grace? You're a priest; I don't expect you to understand. I've gone too far. Father, I'm marked." Ben drew his lips back in a grimace that exposed his long eyeteeth.

"You don't think I understand what it's like to turn my back to God? Benton, I used to worship Satan. I, too, am marked." Father More pushed back his sleeves to reveal silver scars crossing his arms. "I won't talk about that dark idolatry, but I'll tell you about Mrs. Ramirez."

FOURTEEN

"It began when I was a teenager. I guess that's as good a time as any to be a rebel." Father More paused. "Now that *is* an odd thing to say to someone who was a Confederate soldier."

Ben chuckled. "Well, I do understand what you mean."

"If my parents liked it, I didn't. If they wanted me to do something, I wouldn't. If it was popular with kids at school, I did it. Then I found myself involved in a cult." Father More ran his finger over the lines of his scars.

"It was blood they wanted . . . my blood. That was part of the rite. I understand about blood, Benton, I watched enough drip into the sacrificial basin. I didn't care about God. I didn't understand that his pointed finger isn't raised to smite us, but it's beckoning us home. Mrs. Ramirez taught me that . . ."

* * * *

Tom stopped at the window of Ramirez's furniture store and gaped at the sculpture in the window. It was a colored bust of Jesus, crowned with thorns, his eyes turned upward in supplication or agony—Tom wasn't sure which. He was fascinated by a system of fine tubes imbedded in the plastic that trickled some kind of red fluid continuously so the statue seemed to be in a perpetual state of bleeding. He watched, mesmerized by the bizarre artwork.

"It is a miracle, is it not?" A soft voice spoke over his shoulder.

"A miracle? No, I think there's a pump or something inside to circulate the red stuff."

"I am not talking of the statue—it has a pump, you are right. I talk of the Lord Jesus. He is the miracle."

Tom turned around. "You're Mrs. Ramirez."

"And you are Tomás More."

"Thomas—or Tom."

"That is what I said—Tomás."

Tom gave up. "But how do you know who I am?"

"I know your mother, she comes by here all the time. This beautiful store—it belongs to my family. You come inside. I give you something."

"You don't have to give me anything."

"Is nothing. Something I keep for boys like you." She reached under the counter and handed him a small plastic box.

Tom ran his thumb over the words *My Rosary* embossed on the lid. He held up the chain of smooth plastic beads and crucifix.

"You know what this is—beads for praying."

"I know," Tom said.

"I know you know. Your mother tells me you go to some place where they do not think they need these beads for praying. Because they do not pray to Jesus." She touched the tiny figure on the cross. "This is the miracle, Tomás, not the statue with the pump. Do not forget it."

He lowered the beads into the box and snapped the lid.

Mrs. Ramirez went on. "I know you are smart. I see your name on the Honor Roll. But do not think you are more smart than God. That is a mistake."

"You know a lot about me."

"I look out for the boys around here. I pay attention."

He caught her eye. "Do you really? That's more than my parents do. They couldn't care less if I come or go."

"You are wrong. They care."

"How would you know—here in your beautiful furniture store—how could you see into my home? They're never there."

"Your mother tells me. Your father works extra hours—he is tired. Your mother works night shift. They want you to have a better life, so they save for you to go to college."

"Maybe I don't want to go to college. Did they ever ask me?"

"Why do you get good grades then? Good grades you do not tell your friends about?"

"Because . . . I might want to go. I might want the chance."

"But then you cut yourself and cover up the cuts with these things?" She touched the wide leather bands he wore around his wrists.

His mouth dropped open.

"I have seen what they do to people in those underground temples. Do not do it, Tomás. You are a smart boy. You were named after a great man—you could be great too."

"I was named after my grandfather," Tom muttered.

"Oh? Well, maybe he was named after the great man. You could still be great. Come by the church some time. Saturday afternoon they play basketball."

"Maybe," he said, "I'll think about it."

Saturday afternoons were when he met in a friend's basement for their dark rites. Why bounce a ball in the sun when the basement pulsated with a cold, exciting power? Tom dropped the box with the rosary on his dresser.

Sunday morning he lay in a hot tangle of sheets, his arm throbbing from the latest cuts. He felt tormented by the beat of his own heart and finally stumbled out of bed. Feverish and lightheaded, he pressed his palm to his forehead to gauge his temperature, but all he felt was hot.

In the kitchen, he poured a glass of orange juice and peeked under the bandage. His wrist looked red and streaky. Not good. One cut was deeper than usual and seemed to be still oozing blood. Tom wondered if he should have stitches.

"My, you're up early today." His mother began to fill the coffeepot. "Are you okay?"

Tom tried to hide his arm, but his mother saw the bloody wrappings.

"What happened?" She loosened the bandages. "My God, what have you done? Never mind, you don't have to tell me. This needs a doctor. I'll take you to the ER."

"You'll be late for Mass," Tom mumbled as his mother bathed the wounds and wrapped ice and a clean towel around his arm.

She put her hand on the side of his face. "Sweetie, don't you know *you* mean more to me than Mass? Now get your coat."

His mother stayed beside him the whole time, wincing at each prod of the needle and Tom wondered if she felt a deeper pain that he did. Once when the doctor left them alone for a moment she asked if he had tried to kill himself.

"Of course not," he replied with a scowl. "I have to do this. You wouldn't understand."

"You're right, I don't understand. I wish I did." A sob caught in her throat and she wiped her eyes with the back of her hand.

When they got home, she made his bed, smoothing the sheets and plumping the pillows. She gave him Tylenol for his fever, then tucked him in. "Get some sleep." She brushed his forehead with a kiss. As she reached for the light switch, she saw the rosary box on his dresser and opened it, touching the cheap beads.

"Hail Mary, full of grace . . ." her voice faltered.

Tom had heard her say those words a million times.

" . . . Holy Mary, Mother of God, pray for us sinners now and at the hour of our death. Amen."

She held up the crucifix. "Good St. Gerard, protector of the family, watch over us in our troubles. O Sacred Heart of Jesus, guard my son," she whispered. "I love him. In the name of the Father, and of the Son, and of the Holy Ghost. Amen." She crossed herself and slipped the rosary back in the box.

Tom closed his eyes and drifted to sleep . . .

* * * *

"Your mother prayed for you," Benton said.

Father More chuckled. "She still does."

"Mine did, too." Benton unbuttoned his collar and pulled out a small pouch on a cord. He handed it to Father More. "She gave me this when I enlisted. It was her grandmother's. I put it in a leather pouch to protect it from battle. Now I'm the one who's protected."

Father More opened the bag and lifted out the rosary. The wooden beads, worn and polished by years of prayer gleamed softly.

"I can't touch it," Ben went on, "but I promised my mother I'd keep it next to my heart. A promise like that is hard to break."

"It must be comforting to know her prayers are still with you."

"But if she knew what I had become . . ."

"Then her prayers would be more fervent. I think mothers know the farther we are from home, the more we need them."

"And your mother's prayers brought you home?"

"Well, they brought me to church that week . . ."

* * * *

Tom didn't go to the rites that Saturday. He had taken some ribbing from his companions over the professional bandages and he was afraid of what they might do to someone they perceived as a coward. He wandered over to the basketball court instead. He didn't want to play; his wrist was still sore, but he thought he could watch for a while and check it out.

The Catholics in Tom's neighborhood seemed to have graphic taste in religious art. The back wall of the church was covered with a two-story high graffiti-style depiction of the crucifixion. The illustration was detailed and colorful, favoring red, as the artist included quite a bit of gore. Drops fell from the crown of thorns, and a wound gaped in the Christ's chest. Giant nails tore through his hands and feet; slashes and welts covered his gaunt body. Tom gawked.

One of the priests grabbed a towel to wipe his face, and wandered over.

"Hi, I'm Father Julian."

"Tom More."

"Nice to meet you, Tom. I talked to your mom the other day. How's your arm?"

"Okay—I get the stitches out Monday." He pointed to the wall. "I don't get it. This is supposed to be a miracle? Killing an innocent man like that?"

"Crucifixion is a brutal death, don't get me wrong—the miracle came after. His followers wrapped his body and sealed it in a tomb. Three days later, they found the stone rolled away, but when they entered, the tomb was empty. Jesus Christ had risen. One sacrifice for all—*his* body and blood to take away *our* sins. No more of this."

Tom flinched as the priest touched the bandage on his arm.

"I know what goes on underground. Whatever god you worship there is false—let me introduce you to the real one . . ."

* * * *

"And that, as they say, was just the beginning." Father More took a swallow of coffee. "Don't get me wrong—it was a battle. I stopped going to the underground worship, but I still had to fight to stop cutting myself. But by the time I finished high school, I had enrolled in a Catholic college. I earned a BA and a masters in English Literature. By the time I graduated, I knew I was called to the priesthood. But God had a hard ten years of working on me along the way."

"Ten years for you—I've been away one hundred and forty."

"But you have an advantage over me. I strayed before I ever knew our Lord. I went to church, and said all the right words, but it was a while before they became a supplication instead of a recitation. You knew Christ before you fell. You still know him. You have longed to be free of the curse for all these years. If God wanted me, who worshipped the enemy—he certainly wants you. Turn around. The journey home is the shortest one of all."

FIFTEEN

Deirdre locked the green room door and went upstairs to the costume shop. She thought she would use the time before Ben finished work to catch up on a few repairs. She laid the bundle of costumes on the table and opened the box of buttons.

A couple of pairs of shoes needed to be touched up with spray paint. She took them into the dye room so they could dry by the fan while she did the other repairs. A sound from the costume shop caught her attention—the snagging whisper of fabric drawn across the wooden floor.

Someone was in the shop. She hesitated. There was no other way out of the dye room, and if she shut the door she would be cornered. Maybe the old building was just talking in its sleep. She cautiously peeked out the door.

The room was as empty as she left it. But she heard the grate of a shoe and a creaking board. There was nothing to see as she looked around, but nevertheless, she threaded a needle with trembling hands.

A chair scraped across the floor and protested the weight of someone sitting on it. She whipped around. Was that chair pushed in when she came up to the shop? She couldn't be sure. It was pulled out and empty now.

She finished securing the buttons on a jacket and trimmed the knotted thread

"Good evening, Deirdre. You seem nervous. There's no reason to be afraid."

"Sid!" she screamed, feeling his cold breath on her neck. The scissors stuck point down in the floor where she dropped them. "You scared me! How did you get in here?"

He smiled. "I live here . . . at least I do when I'm not with Rhonda. Or hasn't Ben told you about the Enclave?"

"He did, but . . . he said it's not in the theater."

"Oh, my dear, we have been here much longer than the theater—we have always been here." He dangled a bunch of keys from his finger. "And in any case, I have the keys. There was a janitor once who found our lifestyle most intriguing." He licked his lips.

"You're disgusting."

"Oh, *no*, I prefer to think of myself as generous. I'm always happy to share—my body," he paused, flourishing his hand, "or . . . whatever."

Deirdre shuddered. "Why are you stalking me?"

"Stalking? More name-calling? That's not very flattering. How about courting?"

"What do you want?"

"You." He stroked aside a strand of her hair.

Deirdre flinched at his touch. "Why? You already have Rhonda."

"And Count Dracula had three wives. I don't want to limit myself." He glanced at the clock. "Rhonda's expecting me. I don't like to keep her waiting."

"What have you done to her?" Deirdre backed away, moving toward a stack of props.

"Nothing . . . yet. But soon she will beg me to make her a vampire."

"You're lying. She thinks you want to marry her." Deirdre groped in the corner and found a practice sword. Made of heavy wood to simulate the metal ones, use had chipped and blunted the sides, but the end still looked pointed. She lifted it up in front of her face—a talisman, a weapon—then stood *en garde*, racking her memory for those college fencing classes, hoping a wooden sword would prove an effective stake.

"Well, that's interesting. I see you've had some training."

"I have." She sounded braver than she felt.

"Good. A worthy opponent. Go ahead." He ripped his shirt open baring his smooth, pallid chest.

She lowered the sword, aiming for the point beneath his ribcage. She took a deep breath, preparing to lunge.

"But if you slay me, your friend will die."

The sword point wavered. "I don't think so. Ben said she would be restored."

"What does Benton know? I have seduced her—made love to her—that's no secret. And you know I have marked her for my own ends, just as Benton once marked me. I say if you destroy me now, when she is so close, but not yet one of us, she will also die. Can you bear to have her blood on your hands?"

She let the sword fall from her hand and clatter to the floor. "Why don't you leave us alone?"

Sidell buttoned his shirt and tucked it in. "I'm only looking out for everyone's best interests. It's obvious Benton cares for you. What better way could there be than he takes you with him into immortality? And what's good for Benton, is increase for us. Everybody wins."

"Immortality? It would be damnation!"

"Well, that's in the eye of the beholder, isn't it? Personally, I appreciate having no death, no illness, not even an injury that doesn't heal instantly." He picked up the scissors, opened the blades and slashed his wrist. The wound gaped to the bone; blood welled up, filling the cut, splattering the floor with crimson drops. "A pity to waste anything," he said, raising his arm to his mouth. Now his lips were stained and dripping.

Deirdre's stomach heaved and she turned away.

"Look." Sid grabbed her hair, forcing her to face him. The bleeding stopped and the edges of the wound began to knit. They watched it close and fade to a slender line.

He looked at the clock again. "I must go, Rhonda will be wondering where I am. I see you have work to finish and I'm sure you don't want to keep Benton waiting. Until we meet again." He laughed, letting his long, bloodstained teeth show, and then he began to shimmer, like dust in the wind, until he disappeared.

Deirdre sat on the floor amid the bloody splatters and covered her face with her hands. "How can I get myself out of this horror? Sidell is watching everything I do. He's everywhere I turn."

Suddenly the room seemed shadowy and she thought of the empty floors beneath her. And the floors beneath that that were not empty. She shivered.

She fumbled the costumes into a pile and left them on the table. Once she was with Ben, she could relax. She grabbed her purse and headed for the radio station.

The weather had taken a further turn toward spring, and the rain that fell that night had a softer edge; the sidewalks gleamed wetly, but not with the iciness of winter. It was pleasant walking in the dark. The soft evening breeze that smelled of moist earth and green, growing things began to blow away the horrors of the costume shop.

She twined her fingers around Ben's. "Let's go through the cemetery."

He unlatched the well-oiled gate and let her through; it snapped shut behind them.

Deirdre thought about Ben and the sanctuary. "If this is consecrated ground, why can you get in? Isn't there a Guardian here?"

"It's consecrated, true, but as a place for the dead. They have nothing to fear from one of their own—I'm at home here. The church is the place of the Living God—protected from the dead and damned."

The moon threw ghostly shadows across the markers, but they could still read the engraved letters. Benton stopped, hunching his shoulders as he read the words:

Brother, first to leave our band
With life's song as yet unsung
While gray hairs gather on our brows
Thou art forever young.

"That's me. Forever young, forever twenty-three. Everyone I knew has died—my family, my friends— and I'm still here, still the same. Even if the war hadn't taken them, they'd still be dead." His voice grated.

"What happened to them?" Deirdre asked.

"My father was killed at Antietam. My brother was wounded and taken prisoner. He died in prison from infections. The Yankees burned our plantation. The house, barns, outbuildings, everything. I went there— I saw it. Why? Wouldn't it have been more useful as a farm?" Pain chilled his words.

Deirdre had no answer. "I'm sorry, Ben. What happened to your mother?"

"She went to live with her family in Charleston. She died in 1913. I never saw her again. But she had a full life, Deirdre. When she died, she was old. And I'm still young. If it hadn't been for that war . . . I keep asking why?"

"Didn't the slaves have a right to be free?"

"Didn't the slave owners have rights? I'm not saying slavery was good, but that war was bad. So many things died, and yet, I wasn't one of them."

"Rights are important, Benton. They always have been. From the beginning of this country—we have the right to life, liberty and the pursuit of happiness."

"Maybe *you* have those rights. I have no life, no liberty—I'm bound by this curse to maintain my existence by preying on others. Happiness? Any happiness I might find, like a few stolen hours with you, I am destined to destroy by my very nature."

He touched her cheek. "You are so beautiful, but you will grow old, gray-haired, crippled, and I will still be twenty-three."

Deirdre gasped, grabbing his arm. "I heard something—like the click of the gate. What if it's Sid?"

They stopped. Footsteps crunched along the path.

"Let's go." Ben hurried toward the street, his coat swinging behind him.

Deirdre tried to keep up. "Wait." She reached out for his hand, but her fingers slipped away.

The footsteps came faster. Whoever was following kept to the shadows, only the hurried crunch of gravel marked a presence. She gasped for breath and stumbled after him. The steps grew closer.

"Ben," Deirdre screamed. He turned.

A shadowy figure loomed behind Deirdre, one hand curled around her collar, the other clutching a brick overhead. He brought it down with a thunk. Deirdre collapsed.

Benton reached out and grabbed a fistful of shirt, snarling at the attacker. "I could tear your throat out right now, but it isn't worth the effort."

Ben's heightened senses detected a miasma of drink, drugs and diseases that churned his stomach. As he held the whimpering delinquent off the ground, the reek of urine and feces was added to the stench.

"Ugh." Ben threw him against a nearby tomb where he crumpled like a rag to the ground.

Benton kneeled by Deirdre and spoke her name. "Can you hear me?"

He sighed with relief as she moaned and fluttered her eyes. "It's all right, it wasn't Sidell—just a vagrant."

He groped for his cell phone and called 911. Clutching her hand in his, he stated the situation and requested police and an ambulance.

As they transferred her to a stretcher, Deirdre refused to let Benton go. "Don't leave me," she pleaded.

"I won't." With a nod from the attendants, he climbed into the ambulance.

Deirdre would not release Benton's hand even as they wheeled her into a treatment room. "Please stay. I'm scared." Tears trickled down her cheeks.

"You can stay," the nurse agreed. "It's better if she's not upset any more.

Ben remained while they stitched the cut on her head and finally took her to a bed. The doctor assured him she would be fine, but he wanted to observe her overnight.

"You'll be all right now." Ben patted her fingers twined around his. "This hospital is the safest place to be."

"Don't go—there is danger out there tonight."

"I know the streets can be rough, but as you saw tonight, I can handle myself." He tried to smile.

Her mouth turned up. "I *didn't* see. But it's not that kind of danger."

"What do you mean?"

She sighed, turning her head and wincing at the pain. "I don't know. I can hardly think. I feel like something is pressing on my skull. It's a vague danger—something for you. Just stay with me."

"Of course I will." He pushed an armchair next to the bed and sat where he could hold her hand.

A nurse came in with a jug of iced water. She studied Benton as she arranged things on the table. "Are you all right, sir? You look a little pale."

"I'm okay—I always look like this."

"Are you sure? I don't need another patient on my hands. I could bring you a drink if you'd like some coffee or a soda."

"No thank you. I'm fine."

"Very well." She straightened Deirdre's blanket. "Now you should get some sleep. No more talking to this nice young man."

Deirdre giggled as the nurse bustled away. "Do you get that a lot?"

He shrugged. "For the most part I try to avoid hospitals."

"Too many nurses?"

"That—and too much blood. It calls to me."

"Oh, I'm sorry."

"Shh." Benton put his finger to his lips.

"But I can't sleep," she whispered. "My head hurts. They won't give me anything for the pain and I want to talk."

"Then be very quiet." He leaned close to her and smoothed her hair off her face.

"That feels good; your hands are so nice and cool."

"That's because I'm dead," he whispered.

"I forgot." She kissed his fingers. "I love you anyway."

It was close to morning when the nurse returned. "Haven't you slept at all?"

"What time is it?" Deirdre asked.

"About five o'clock," she answered, popping a thermometer in Deirdre's mouth and taking her pulse.

After the nurse had gone, Deirdre stretched in the bed and yawned. "I feel a lot better. The pressure on my head has gone. You could go home if you want."

"I'll stay as long as you need me."

"The danger is over; I felt it lift. I think I could even get some sleep now. The sun isn't up yet—you should go before it rises."

Ben squeezed her hand. "I don't mind staying."

"I know that—thanks. But everything will be okay now. I can tell."

"Give me a call when it's time to go and I'll bring a taxi to pick you up."

"Ben, you are so sweet." She pulled his head close to hers and kissed his forehead. "I'll see you later."

SIXTEEN

Deirdre cuddled under a quilt on her couch while Ben puttered in the kitchen. Shelley had stopped by with a pot of chicken soup and a batch of chocolate chip cookies to tell Deirdre to take a few days off work. All she wanted to do was lie on the sofa.

"I just want some soup," she called. "I'm not very hungry."

"I thought some coffee would be nice with those cookies," he replied.

"Mmm, it smells wonderful. Good idea."

As he brought hot soup and a plate of cheese and crackers, they heard a knock at the door. She took the food. "Better see who it is."

"It's Lieutenant Bowen, miss. May I have a word with you?"

"Of course," she called. "Let him in, Ben."

Benton opened the door.

"I apologize for bothering you, Miss Maguire. I know you spent last night in the hospital, but I need to verify some times concerning the incident. I'd appreciate it if Mr. Colyer would stay—he can confirm them as well."

"Have a seat." Deirdre pointed to a chair. "You don't mind if we eat, do you?"

"Not at all." He pulled out a notebook. "Just tell me where you were last night."

"All right." She sipped some soup. "I got to work about six-fifteen—the stage manager saw me come in, and he locked up around eleven. Sometimes I leave when he does, but I planned to meet Ben at midnight and I wanted to finish some work."

"Do you have a key?"

"Only to the costume shop—the rest of the doors are set so you can get out, but they lock behind you."

"I see." He made a note. "When did you leave the theater?"

"Eleven-thirty. I got to the radio station about ten minutes later. The guard should have my name on the sign-in sheet."

"He does. He says you and Mr. Colyer left shortly after midnight. Did you pass anyone on the street?"

"I think we waved to the bartender at Mickey's—I mean, we usually do. After we started through the graveyard, things get a little fuzzy for me. I don't know what time it was when I was attacked. But Ben was with me all the way to the hospital."

"Yes, we have the time he called in the police report—twelve twenty-two. Do you have anything to add, Mr. Colyer?"

"That sounds about right. Only a minute or two passed from the attack until I made the call. I think I roughed up the perp a little, though."

Lt. Bowen smiled. "I'll say. He was admitted shortly after Miss Maguire. He opted not to press any charges." He looked at his pad. "How long were you at the hospital with Miss Maguire?"

"I stayed all night."

"Can anyone verify that?"

Ben nodded. "I never left Deirdre's room. The nurse was in and out, she would probably remember. I finally came home after five. I took a cab—you could find the driver."

"Do you have any enemies, Mr. Colyer?"

Ben shrugged. "My radio show is quite popular—I suppose I could have professional rivals."

"Anyone who would kill to take you out of the picture?"

"What do you mean?"

"Last night a young woman was found with her throat cut." Lt. Bowen slid a photograph across the table. "I know the picture is not a pretty sight, but can you identify her?"

Deirdre gasped. "Oh, no, it's Rhonda—Rhonda Petrie."

"I understand she also worked at the Union Square Theater."

Nodding, Deirdre reached for a tissue and blew her nose. "She was a good friend of mine."

"I'm very sorry to have to bring such bad news. My condolences, miss."

"Thank you, Lieutenant."

Lieutenant Bowman continued. "Mr. Colyer, evidence found at the scene points to you."

Benton frowned. "May I ask what sort of evidence?"

"A black silk scarf and a time clock swipe card. The guard at the radio station identified both of them as yours. However, if your alibi checks out, it proves you could not have been involved. So I ask, who would want to see you convicted of murder?"

"Murder . . . Who indeed." Ben fixed his eyes on the lieutenant, while his fingers dug into the arms of the chair and his soup congealed in the bowl.

"I realize there are people in this world who do things like this for the headlines. I hope this isn't one of those cases. If you think of anyone—anything at all, let me know." He handed them each a business card. "Thank you for your time. I'll let myself out."

As the door shut behind the lieutenant, Ben lowered his head onto his hands. "Only a vampire could have obtained evidence like that."

Deirdre frowned. "Why didn't you tell him about Sidell?"

Ben raised his hands in helplessness. "What would be the point? The undead are un-people. Could you find him? Do you know where he lives?"

"Wait." She rubbed her face. "He told me he lives at the theater—in the Enclave—when he's not with Rhonda."

"I'm sure the police have been to Rhonda's house—no doubt they've searched it carefully. Does it sound like Sidell was there?" Ben's voice grew harsh. "Do you know where the door to the Enclave is? Could you direct the police to it?"

"I—I don't know, Ben, I guess I couldn't."

"Deirdre, this is beyond Lieutenant Bowen's area. Think about it. I died during a war over a century ago—my mother got a telegram from the Army. I have to build up an identity in order to work—all false of course, and I have to move and change my name from time to time. We never age, remember.

"Sidell passed out of this life—a drug addict, a whore, missing and presumed dead. No one tried to trace him then. There is no way to trace him now—no social security number, no utility bills, no door to the Enclave. Vampires don't *need* doors!"

Deirdre drew in a breath. "The duct work."

"Yes—that and the abandoned sewers. It *is* possible for mortals to enter the Enclave if they know where to go. But suppose the police did find him? No cell could hold him. Imagine if they tried to execute him for murder."

Deirdre shuddered at the thought of Sidell, a lethal overdose of toxic chemicals coursing through his veins, calmly rising up from the chair, laughing in the faces of the executioners. She clenched her fists. "What can we do?"

He took her hands; pain mixed with hope in his eyes. "I can't do it—it's up to you."

She swallowed. "A stake?"

"A stake."

"What about his body? I don't exactly need a murdered corpse on my hands."

"Don't worry. He'll disintegrate—to bones, maybe, or dust. I've seen it happen."

"And would that happen to you?" Her eyes widened.

"If I'm destroyed, yes, it would."

"But what if you're restored?"

He shrugged. "I don't know. *That* I have never seen happen." He reached for a package and handed it to her. "This is for Sidell. It's up to you to stop him now."

Deirdre looked at the stake, thick, heavy and sharpened to a point at one end. "You knew it would come to this."

"Yes, I thought it would. Even before Rhonda's death."

"I'll try." She bit her lip. "I don't know how brave I am, though."

"You are brave, Deirdre. It will be enough. There is a legend of the slayers—those born to be paladins of the light. The power sleeps deep within them until it's needed, then it wells up into the light. When the time comes, they meet one of the masters, teachers versed in the lore of the dark forces."

"Father More?"

"Yes. He's clearly a master. Remember all the books you said he has? The two of you were brought together for this time. I think you might be one of the slayers."

A slayer? Deirdre thought of Sidell standing with his shirt open and her sword pointing at his breast. If not for Rhonda, she could have done it. If he hadn't lied, she would have pierced his heart. She looked up at Ben, her mouth set in determination. "Where do we find him?"

"I'll show you. The best time to slay him will be noon—when he is asleep and his powers are weakest. Unfortunately, my powers are weakest then, too, and I won't be able to help you get in. We'll have to enter the Enclave just before sunrise. It will be safer, and there's less chance we'll run into anyone working in the kitchens. Then we'll wait until mid-day when you can go on to the lairs."

"Ben, will I have to crawl through the ductworks?"

"Don't worry, there are many ways to the Enclave." He put his arms around her. "You won't go in alone."

SIXTEEN

Benton dressed for work, his clothes the usual monochromatic shades. He considered himself one who walked each day in Death's dreamscape, and colors like blue or green—colors of the daylight—were more suited to living things. He pulled on black jeans and a gray polo shirt.

He had been brought up wearing fine linen and cotton shirts, brocaded silk and soft woolens and he appreciated the smooth cotton knit and how it felt across his shoulders. His heavy overcoat wasn't suited to the stormy weather so he chose a trench coat of suede microfiber appealing to his sense of touch, luxurious to his hand, but repelling the rain more efficiently than the stiff waxed canvas Ben remembered from other years. Rain or shine, summer or winter he always wore the same hat with the brim pulled down to his eyes.

Ben started across town toward the cathedral. Father More had talked about hope. Rain sluiced through the gutters and dripped off his hat. Could he

151

offer that hope to Benton? He said that God welcomes the return of all his prodigals, no matter how dark the path they had walked. His path had been dark indeed. Ben splashed through an unavoidable puddle. Maybe Father More would have time to talk before he had to be at work.

The rectory looked like a private home—Ben wondered if he could enter. He was encouraged by the fact that he got close enough to press the doorbell.

"Hi. Can I help you?" A teenaged boy answered the door.

Benton stepped into the vestibule—so far, no barrier. "I'd like to see Father More."

The boy turned and yelled. "Hey, Father, someone wants to see ya."

Father More came to the door. "Benton, what a pleasure, come right in."

Ben paused, an eyebrow raised in question.

"My office is downstairs and quite public. You can enter." The priest held the door wide.

Benton stepped over the threshold with a sigh of relief and followed Father More to his study. After sending the boy to the kitchen for some tea, Father More indicated a chair and sat down himself. "Make yourself at home."

Ben examined the collection of literature that he had heard so much about. "Deirdre said you were well-read. I've been thinking—I believe she might have the gifting of a vampire slayer. But each slayer has a teacher—a master. I think you might be hers."

Father More leaned back in his chair. "Well, I do have two degrees."

Ben looked over the framed diplomas. "Yes, I see that. It's an odd coincidence, isn't it?"

"I never discount odd coincidences. So I have to admit, the thought had crossed my mind. And I have something else." Father More unlocked the bottom drawer of his desk. "Deirdre hasn't seen this. I keep it locked up because it may be valuable—at any rate, it's very old. It's not something to share with the general public."

He lifted out a heavy book bound in tooled leather, moved aside some clutter and laid it on the desk. The gold-leafed title was a single word: Vampyr.

Ben leaned over to inspect the volume. "Where did you get this?"

"At an auction about five years ago. It's a strange story. I stopped to browse, but I hadn't planned on buying anything. I decided to bid because this book looked interesting—I'm not a collector of incunabula as a rule. But a fifteenth century vampire hunter's handbook was hard to resist." Father More smiled.

"Well, I can see how you would have been tempted," Ben agreed, "but I'd think a book like this would be quite pricey."

"Yes, I thought so, too. I set myself a limit so I wouldn't get carried away in the heat of the moment, but after two or three bids, the others dropped out. I got it for $99.00. My limit was $100.00." Father More leaned back in his chair.

Ben raised an eyebrow. "Clearly it was intended for you. Talismans like this have a way of finding those who need them. Have you read it?"

"Some of it." Father More opened the book. "Look at this."

The first page had only a poem. Benton read the words out loud:

Beware, if you would wander here,
A path beset with evil.
Only the pure in heart may wield
These arms against the devil.

Father More nodded. "This is a common warning. A caution, I believe to those who might be susceptible to corruption." He turned the page.

The second page was covered in illustrations and symbols. Intertwined leaves and vines seemed to form a cross in the center of the page and Benton could make out a lion and an eagle. He thought one of the figures was a bull. As he put out a finger to trace an angel's wing, there was a flash, like an electric arc. He snatched away his hand and stumbled backwards, tripping over a chair.

"Are you all right?" Father More extended a helping hand.

"I think so." Benton lay stunned on the carpet, cradling his red and blistering fingers.

"Oh dear," Father More said touching his wrist, "that burn needs ice."

"No." Benton gasped. "I'll be fine. Just give me a minute." He sat up and flexed his fingers. "What happened?"

"I was hoping you'd tell me. This page is covered with Christian symbols—I think the book must have been anointed with sacred oil or soaked with holy water."

"Well, that would keep me from touching it." Benton stood up and held his now healed hand to Father More.

"Put the book away. I don't need to see any more. After all, I do know how to slay a vampire." He curled his mouth in a grimace that showed his long teeth. "You have to show it to Deirdre. She's going to need you if I'm . . ."

"If you're . . . gone?" Father More asked. "Is that what you came to see me about?"

"Yes. I'm ready to seek reconciliation with the Father of us all."

A knock at the door heralded the arrival of tea and Benton found a chair while Father More passed him a steaming mug. He sipped, gathering his thoughts. It was strangely difficult to begin. He was thankful that Father More knew most of the story already. "A young woman was killed the other day—Rhonda Petrie. She was Deirdre's friend."

"Yes, I heard about it on the news. Apparently the police have no leads." Father More stirred his drink.

"Not so. They have evidence. It led them straight to me. Fortunately I had an alibi."

"Iron clad?

Benton smiled. "More like scrub-suited. I was at the hospital with Deirdre. She made me stay. She had a . . . premonition, I guess you could call it. At any rate, the nurses can vouch for me."

"That's good."

"It's good for me. But, there is a problem, Father." Benton frowned. "I know who did it. Sidell Prentiss."

Father More shrugged. "Why is that a problem? Call Lieutenant Bowman and turn him in."

"I could, but he's another vampire. I can't even prove he exists." Benton jumped up and began to pace. "The lieutenant is no fool. How could I turn Sidell in?"

"As you said, that *is* a problem. What next?" Father More tapped a pen against a pad of paper. "Is there anything I can do?"

Ben turned, crossed his arms and leaned against the desk. "Sidell has to be destroyed. I talked to Deirdre—she is willing to do it."

"She's a brave girl."

"That she is. I believe she's the one—I could see the resolve in her eyes as she agreed. She *will* accept the role of slayer. She is strong, Father More, but she needs you. Can you accept your role as master?"

"Master?" Father More stroked the worn leather of the old volume. "I clearly seem to be suited for the part. I've done the research, as it were." He glanced at the framed diplomas and the shelves of books. "And I'm here at the time and place of need—trained to battle the forces of evil."

He looked at Benton, holding his eyes, then sighed and drank some tea. "Yes, Benton, I accept the role of master."

Benton echoed the sigh. "Good." He sank into an armchair. "Will you also watch over her as a sister? She has no family here, and she shouldn't be alone."

"Of course I will. But what of you? She considers you a friend."

"I feel like I am at a threshold, Father, and I can't see past the door. I don't know what lies ahead for me. But I do know this—there is no gray area for me anymore. If my being puts someone in jeopardy, whether it's someone I care about or not, I must choose. And my choice is to throw my lot in with the vampires, or to follow the way of Christ."

"Then which do you choose?"

"I'm seeking reconciliation, Father. I choose Christ. I am un-dead, but I choose life."

"Are you prepared to make confession?"

"Yes." Ben shoved his fingers into his tousled hair. "I made a list."

"That's a good start."

"It's very long."

"I'm not surprised. I have time, Benton, take as long as you need. May God, who has enlightened every heart, help you to know your sins and trust in his mercy."

Benton pulled a sheaf of papers out of his pocket and unfolded it. "Bless me, Father, for I have sinned. I cannot count the years since my last confession."

He paused, drawing in a breath, then reached for his cup and gulped the last of his tea. Father More smiled encouragement, and Benton began the recitation. When he came to the end, he crumpled the papers into his fist and looked up. "My God, my life is in your hands, to keep it or end it. I will do your will. In the name of your precious Son, amen."

He held out the paper wad and looked around. "I wish I could burn this," he said.

Father More held out a wastebasket and Benton crammed it in. He bowed his head onto his folded hands, tears he hadn't felt for decades filling his eyes.

Father More put his hand on Benton's head. "God, the Father of mercies, through the death and resurrection of his Son has reconciled the world to himself and sent the Holt Spirit among us for the forgiveness of sins. Through the ministry of the Church may God give you pardon and peace, and I absolve you of your sins in the name of the Father, and of the Son and of the Holy Spirit. Amen."

"Thank you," Benton whispered.

"I will pray for you and Deirdre tomorrow. Both of you come when you're done with Sidell, and I'll celebrate Mass for you."

"We will. Good night, Father."

"Good night. God be with you."

Benton turned, before he walked into the shadows he had grown to love, to look at Father More. He stood framed in the glowing light from the hallway and raised his hand to wave.

Benton waved in return. He looked up at the sky—dark overhead and crusted with stars, but still a deep blue at the horizon—and smiled at the handwriting of a loving God.

SEVENTEEN

Deirdre huddled in the doorway outside the rear entrance to the Athenaeum, the wooden stake an awkward weight in her shoulder bag. A sharpened piece of wood seemed an odd sort of weapon for this modern age. Most action heroines carried Uzis and throwing knives.

She chuckled at the thought of herself in such a role. Of course, she couldn't carry a nail file on an airplane, but she would probably be able to get a stake past the security checks. It might pique the interest of the X-ray technician but it wouldn't set off the metal detectors.

Right now her job was to watch the alley for any passersby. No one came through the silent street. Not even a stray cat investigated the leftover puddles. This was a dead time—no longer night and not yet morning.

Ben handed her the flashlight and pulled on a pair of gloves. With a job of breaking and entering to do, a vampire came in handy. Shimmering like stardust, he dematerialized his body, sifting through the gap in the doorframe. He unlocked the door from the inside. She sidled through and he secured the door behind her. Ben left no mark on the door, not a scratch or fingerprint. Unless they set off the fire alarm, no one would know they were there.

Away from the grandly decorated lobby of the theater and the elegant restaurant area, the halls of the Athenaeum were shabby. The old wood floors were covered with a fraying gray tweed carpet runner. The walls, once painted a merely murky green, had darkened with time to the color of sludge and absorbed the beam from the flashlight. A wide staircase loomed up into the gloom, the banisters casting tree-like shadows on the walls. Familiar territory to Deirdre, it led to the theater's administrative offices. Ben took her to the other side of the hall.

"Downstairs," he whispered, his lips brushing her hair. She followed him down the creaking stairs, through the silent kitchens. Here the gleaming stainless steel fixtures threw back the flashlight's beam and she jumped as it picked up the shiny outline of a cleaver suspended over the counter along with a rack of knives.

They tiptoed into a storeroom fragrant with stacked food supplies. Ben stopped in front of what looked like a built-in shelf unit. Counting, he marked off three shelves down from the top and three boards from the left. He pushed his finger into a knothole, and the whole section of wall rotated.

They stepped through the opening into a dismal office. A few bits of moldering furniture competed with rodent droppings for the room.

Deirdre grimaced with disgust. "How did a place like this get here?"

"It was part of the foundation of the original building that stood on this spot." Ben played the light around the walls. "I think bootleggers remodeled it during Prohibition when they needed to hide contraband."

Deirdre kicked aside a tattered paper dated 1933. "It looks like they haven't used it since that amendment was repealed. They haven't cleaned anything since then anyway. Besides, it's not convenient unless you want to hide."

"Or if you're part of the Enclave. We can wait here—there's a sofa."

"You must be kidding—I don't want to sit on that. It's revolting." Deirdre shuddered.

The flashlight revealed tufts of stuffing protruding from the shabby armrests, the back streaked with dark, indeterminate stains, and the cushions sagging dispiritedly. The odor of mousy mildew enhanced the morbid décor.

"It doesn't get any better farther on—just closer to the Enclave. It'll be okay. I'll spread out my coat—we can sit on that. Unless you prefer the floor."

"Ugh—no thanks." Who knew how many species of feet had trod those filthy boards? "I guess the sofa will have to do."

Ben put his arm around her and she snuggled next to him. "You should get some sleep. It's going to be a busy day."

"Right." She looked up at him. "You won't freak out suddenly while I'm sleeping and decide to . . ." She touched her neck.

"Absolutely not. Dawn is coming. I have to sleep too."

Deirdre tucked her feet up on the sofa and leaned against Benton's chest. She never felt warmth from his body, but she drew comfort from him all the same. Would they ever have normal times sitting together like this—watching a movie and eating popcorn? A moldy basement was not her idea of a normal setting. She sighed and shifted her weight, trying to find a comfortable spot in the sagging cushions.

Ben cupped her chin in his hand and looked into her eyes. "I won't prey on you, dear, but I *can* help you sleep."

"Glamour?"

He nodded. "Yes. Shhh. All you have to do is close your eyes." In spite of her apprehension of the coming day, she drifted easily into dreamless sleep.

Benton woke her a few hours later. "Time to get moving."

The next door was a worm-eaten wooden panel. Deirdre helped him slide it open on surprisingly well-oiled rollers. Steps led further underground.

He pointed. "That's the way." They headed back to the shabby office.

"You're on your own now," Ben whispered. "I can't go down there, but I'll wait here for you. And Deirdre . . ."

She looked up.

"When Sidell is dead, I'm going to talk to Father More. I made my confession and I'm prepared, even if I can't get into the church."

"Good." Deirdre nodded and drew out the stake. It felt heavy in her hand—smooth and lethal. She handed her bag to Benton. He took it and pressed a quick kiss to her forehead.

They had planned every step from here so they would not need to use words. Deirdre wiped her sweat-dampened fingers and clutched the stake firmly in one hand and the flashlight in the other. Walking as softly as she could, she started down the stairs.

At one step, a rat squealed as she trod on his tail and she bit her lip to restrain the squeal that rose in her own throat. With heart pounding, she paused. The rat hustled into a crack in the wall and she let out the pent-up breath she hadn't realized she was holding.

The walls gleamed in the dim glow of the flashlight with some kind of seepage, and the hall smelled like the earth of a graveyard—aged and rotting. She tried not to imagine what might make that stench.

Beyond the stairs stretched a hall that reminded her of a dormitory of graves. How many undead lay slumbering behind those doors and curtains?

At the bottom of the stairs, she stopped, and looked back. Ben pointed again, and held up two fingers. She nodded. Sidell's was the second door. He gave her a sign of encouragement and faded into the shadows.

Deirdre pushed aside the curtain to a tiny cell. Draperies shrouded the walls, oddly ornate colors and textures that gave the room the quality of a richly padded casket. Sidell reclined on a velvet-draped cot. With his cruel eyes veiled in slumber, he seemed almost angelic. His beauty enthralled her—black eyelashes fanned ivory cheeks, silky blonde hair framed an exquisite face. His slender hands lay loosely clasped on his breast, barely rising and falling with each breath. His skin gleamed pale as marble. The points of his vampire teeth glinting on his crimson lips were the only sign of corruption.

He seemed asleep, but she thought a glimmer sparked from under his eyelids.

"Now or never, girl." She drew in a deep breath.

She raised the stake above her head, stepped closer, and thrust at his chest. Suddenly his eyes flew open and, snarling, he grabbed for her with hooked talon fingers.

Too late.

As she plunged the stake into his flesh, a shrill screech whistled from his gaping mouth. Scarlet blood fountained from his heart, soaking the draperies, pooling on the floor beneath the cot as his body crumpled. Silvery blue eyes stared at her, now blank and sightless. Even before his cry faded, the crumpled shell of his body deteriorated into a pile of discolored bones.

Deirdre gasped for breath as she stepped away from the spreading blood.

Was someone coming? Sidell made enough noise to wake the dead. *And they are dead.* She backed into the hallway as the curtain of the cell next to Sidell's opened. Gnarled fingers gripped the fabric, and she flashed her light into hollow eyes. Deirdre shrieked and raised the dripping stake. The hand withdrew into the shadow. Without a backward glance, she sprinted for the stairs, the doorway and the safety of the mouse-ridden storeroom where Ben waited with outstretched arms.

EIGHTEEN

"He said he'd be here." Deirdre paced across the stone steps of the cathedral.

"Then we'll wait." Father More shoved his hands in his trousers pockets and leaned against the wrought-iron railing.

The sun had begun to set, casting a rosy glow over the pedestrians and gilding the flock of pigeons pecking for crumbs along the sidewalk. She turned and looked over the plaza once more, this time spotting Ben's distinctive black clad figure easily as he strode through the crowd. "There he is." She let out a sigh of relief.

"Run and meet him, child."

She grinned at Father More as she hurried down the steps.

Ben kept his back to the sun; his hat pulled down to shade his eyes. "I can feel the power of the vampire awaken in me as the sun sets. This is the time of day I grow strong. I shouldn't have come."

"I'm glad you did." She slipped her hand into Ben's.

"I wanted to." He slowed down as they neared the imposing edifice of the church with its glowing windows and ranks of watching saints above the doors. "What if the door is still barred?"

"I think Father More has an idea." Deirdre gestured his way; Father More raised a hand in greeting.

"Wait." Benton paused, pulling back on her hand, and she turned to see what he wanted. He smoothed aside an escaping strand of her hair with trembling fingers and whispered, "I'm frightened."

"I know." She looked up into his pale, solemn face—wanting to kiss him, to make this a tender moment—but he seemed distracted.

"Before we go in, I have something I want to give you." He took a small wrapped package out of his pocket.

She peeled the tissue off an antique silver frame holding a picture of a Confederate soldier. She glanced from Ben's face to the cocky recruit in the photograph and back again. "This looks . . . like you!"

"It *is* me. A travelling photographer took it shortly after I enlisted. My mother wanted one, and this one I saved for my girl, if I ever had one." He chuckled, then grew serious. "I don't know what will happen in there," he nodded toward the church, "and I wanted you to have something to remember me by. I couldn't have a modern picture taken—you know vampires don't register on film." He touched the smiling face of the young soldier. "I haven't changed much."

"You haven't changed at all." Even his curly shoulder length hair looked the same. "Tell me something. Is Benton Colyer your real name?"

"Yes, it is. It says differently on my ID cards—I have to change them periodically—but Benton Colyer is usually my professional name. I suppose it's foolish, but I happen to like my name."

"I couldn't think of you as anything but Ben—I'm glad that's really you. This is a treasure. Thank you."

"My pleasure." He drew in a breath as if to gather strength from the air.

She took his hand again. "Come on. I think we've kept Father More waiting long enough." As they walked through the pigeons, the birds rose, clattering and scolding around them, then settled back to the crumbs.

Deirdre and Benton mounted the steps, but Ben struggled, taking each one slower than the one before. Finally he stopped a few feet outside the church door. As if an energy field kept him at a distance, he could stand near the door, but not reach it. Sweat beaded his forehead as he tried to take a closer step.

Ben put out his hand. Deirdre and Father More watched him press against a barrier they couldn't see, but he could feel. In spite of the pain, his hands groped and pressed like a street performer miming a box. The muscles in his neck strained with the obvious effort.

Gasping, he stopped. "I don't think I could pass through and survive. And if I did, that would profane the holy place." He covered his face with his burned hands. "Can't you see? Even God is protected from those like me."

Deirdre laid her hands on Benton's shoulders.

Father More moved around them and opened the door. "Please come in, Benton," he said. "You are welcome here. I am extending an invitation."

Ben took a deep breath and forced himself through the field. Deirdre could see blue static surge and crackle around him as he finally breached the barrier.

He caught his breath and rolled his shoulders as if to unclench the muscles. "It was a Guardian," he whispered as he gazed around the sanctuary. "I *am* welcome here."

"What exactly is a Guardian?" Deirdre asked.

"I'm not sure--they're not sacred entities. He shrugged. "One surrounded this church."

"The Guardians are spirits—dark forces to keep you out, not to protect the church. I should have realized." Father More shook his head. "The evil ones don't want you to return to the light."

"But I'm here."

"Yes. As St. Paul says: 'For we wrestle not against flesh and blood, but against principalities, against powers, against the rulers of the darkness of this world, against spiritual wickedness in heavenly places.' The rulers of darkness may try, but in the end they will not win."

"I'm ready to stop fighting, Father."

Father More beamed. "Good. In that case, why don't you take off your coat? We have some more to talk about."

"Like my penance," Ben agreed.

"Go ahead, I'll sit here." Deirdre folded her coat over the back of a pew and sat down. Ben left his things with her and followed Father More.

Deirdre took out the photograph. This was the man she loved—the man she had seen looking out of the vampire's eyes. Would she someday be his wife?

Wordlessly, she sent a petition. God knew what was best for Benton. After all, he was God's child—his wayward child. "I know you want him back, but can't I have him too? You know I love him." She pressed the picture to her heart and bowed her head. "But we will do your will."

After a few moments, she pulled out her rosary and sought solace in the well-known prayers. She had spoken from her heart, now she spoke from memory, trusting the words to find their way to the feet of Jesus, soothed by the repetition of the litany.

"Eternal Father, I offer you the Body and Blood, soul and Divinity of your dearly beloved Son, our Lord, Jesus Christ in atonement for our sins and those of the whole world.

"For the sake of his sorrowful Passion, have mercy on us and on the whole world. O my Jesus, forgive us of our sins. Save us from the fires of hell. Lead all souls into heaven, especially those in most need of thy mercy." Deirdre closed her eyes. "Especially Benton."

Ben slid into the pew and wrapped his arm around her. She nestled close to him, putting her head on his chest and he smoothed her hair.

"Father More is going to celebrate Mass for us. He'll be back in a minute."

"Are you ready?"

"Yes. I've waited too long." He grinned and she thought his vampire teeth seemed less noticeable. "I wouldn't be here if it weren't for you. Thank you, Deirdre."

"Anyone could have done what I did." She tipped her head back and returned his smile.

"But no one else ever got close enough," he said. "No one else ever saw the man behind the vampire. And maybe there was no one else I would have trusted anyway. I don't know what will come to pass now, but I'm thankful to have come this far."

Father More prepared the table and lit the candles. He beckoned and they knelt side by side at the altar. Ben took Deirdre's hand and they bowed their heads as the priest began.

"In the name of the Father, and of the Son, and of the Holy Spirit."

"Amen," they responded.

"Lord, we have sinned against you: show us your mercy and love."

"And grant us your salvation."

Father More said, "May almighty God have mercy on us, forgive us our sins, and bring us to everlasting life."

"Amen," they all answered.

Then he read from the Gospel according to Luke. "I will break away and return to my father, and will say to him, Father, I have sinned against God and against you; I no longer deserve to be called your son."

The last rays of the setting sun illumined the window illustrating the Prodigal Son and cast shards of colored light on the floor around them.

"We believe in one God, the Father, the Almighty, maker of heaven and earth, of all that is seen and unseen . . ."

Deirdre's voice joined the others in the familiar words rejoicing as she spoke them in the accomplishment Ben had made in being here beside her.

"Lift up your hearts," spoke Father More.

"We lift them up to the Lord," they answered.

"Let us give thanks to the Lord our God."

"It is right to give him thanks and praise."

Here they were, side by side in this peace filled sanctuary, preparing to partake of Communion. Silently Deirdre added her own thanks for that miracle. She looked up at Father More.

He said, "Let us proclaim the mystery of faith: Dying you destroyed our death, rising you restored our life. When we eat this bread and drink this cup, we proclaim your death, by your cross and resurrection, you have set us free. Lord Jesus, come in glory."

Now again the three voices joined: "Our Father, who art in heaven . . ."

"This is the Lamb of God who takes away the sins of the world. Happy are those who are called to his supper."

Deirdre felt Ben's grip on her hand tighten as they answered, "Lord, I am not worthy to receive you, but only say the word and I shall be healed."

Father More presented the elements—the simple bread and wine that had now become the body and blood of the Savior. "The Body of our Lord Jesus Christ which was given for thee . . ."

"Amen." Deirdre let the wafer melt on her tongue. Ben still held her hand and raised his face in expectation as he took his wafer.

Father More lifted the chalice. "The Blood of our Lord Jesus Christ, which was shed for thee, preserve thy body and soul unto everlasting life . . ."

"His blood, Ben," she gasped as she realized the significance of this feast for her friend. "This is the blood you need."

She drank and Father More passed the cup to Ben. His hand trembled as he guided the cup to his lips. She watched his throat work as he swallowed the wine.

Then he jerked, convulsing as if a jolt of electricity had passed through his frame. His back arched and he grabbed the altar rail, then hung, gasping as the current ebbed.

Deirdre tentatively touched his arm, almost expecting a shock to run through her fingers. Instead, she felt warmth radiate through his body. As she watched, a rosy tint suffused his skin.

"Ben, are you all right?" she whispered.

"I'm okay," he looked at the priest. "Go on."

Father More began the benediction. "May the peace of God, which passes all understanding . . ."

For a long moment they knelt in silence absorbing that unfathomable peace.

"The Mass is ended. Go in peace."

Benton turned to Deirdre, his face alight with joy. "Did I ever tell you how much I care about you?"

"No."

"Well, I do." He put his arms around her. "I love you, Deirdre. You brought me to life."

She embraced him, sharing his happiness, pressing her cheek to his and feeling the energy pulse in his veins. But even as she felt it, his heartbeat seemed to slow.

She held him tightly, but after a moment she realized she was supporting most of his weight. She tried to hold him up, but he overbalanced and slipped to the floor, rolling onto his back as he fell. She crawled to his side and he turned his head and reached for her.

"Can you hear me?" She grabbed his hand. "Ben, say something."

"I am free." He smiled and no vampire fangs marred his looks. "Amen."

"Help him, Father," Deirdre pleaded. "I think he's dying."

Pushing back the sleeves of his robes, Father More ran to Ben's side. He felt for a pulse, first in Ben's wrist, then his neck.

"I'll try CPR." He breathed air into Ben's lungs, pressed on his chest, breathed and pressed, intent on the rhythm. Ben's head lolled, rolling from side to side, his eyes white slits. The minutes dragged as he continued the treatment, but Ben was unresponsive. Finally Father More stopped and sat back.

"I'm sorry, Deirdre, I'm afraid he's gone. At least we know he's with the Lord."

He looked at her, his eyes glistening. "I have to call 911—you stay here with Ben."

Tears filled her eyes and spilled over. She took Ben's hand and pressed it to her cheek. His newly warmed skin slowly grew cool, now the lifeless fingers hung slack in her grasp, and she laid them across his chest. Peace bathed his face in final repose, his gray eyes sightless, staring up, beyond the confines of the church. She pressed her fingers on his eyelids and closed them. A silent scream tore her heart apart. More than anything she wanted to lie next to Ben, holding him, feeling his arms around her. Her happy ending was not for this world. She wiped her eyes with her hand and gathered strength from the peace-filled sanctuary.

She gently kissed Ben's cooling lips. "Till we meet again, my love, on the other side of the river."

The sound of sirens tore the quiet of the evening. Tires crunched to a stop outside and footsteps pounded up the steps. The church door swung open and Lieutenant Bowman led his men into the sanctuary. Deirdre sat motionless next to Ben in a fading pool of colored sunlight.

Father More hurried forward to greet the police. "Thank you for coming so quickly."

"We were coming anyway." Lieutenant Bowman opened his notebook. "I have a few questions I need to ask Benton Colyer. A neighbor said he might be here."

Father More shook his head. "I'm sorry, Lieutenant. I'm afraid he is no longer with us."

"He's . . . dead?" He looked from the priest to the motionless body on the floor.

"Yes." Father More answered.

The lieutenant continued. "Do you know how?"

"As far as I can tell, the causes were natural—heart failure I suppose."

Deirdre stood up. "I'm sorry, Lieutenant. You came too late." But she couldn't resist the upwelling of joy that lifted her heart. The timing had been perfect for Ben.

"Yes. It's out of my jurisdiction now." He flipped the notebook closed and slid it into his pocket. "I was hoping for a lead in Rhonda Petrie's murder. We have no suspect, but the case will remain open."

Deirdre stood up. Lieutenant Bowen would be hearing more from her. Deirdre knew what lay beneath the town and even suspected there were other open cases she could help resolve. Some secrets needed to see the light of day.

She squared her shoulders as she remembered the way the smooth wood of the stake felt in her hand.

I am the slayer.

ACKNOWLEDGEMENTS

There always a few people who need thanks:

West Branch Christian Writers, my fabulous and fun critique group
Lisa Lickel, my editor
Father Weary for his insights on being a priest
Larry Weidman who told me about being a radio host
Tonya Wilhelm for her beautiful cover art. You can find her work at www.wilhelm-photography.com